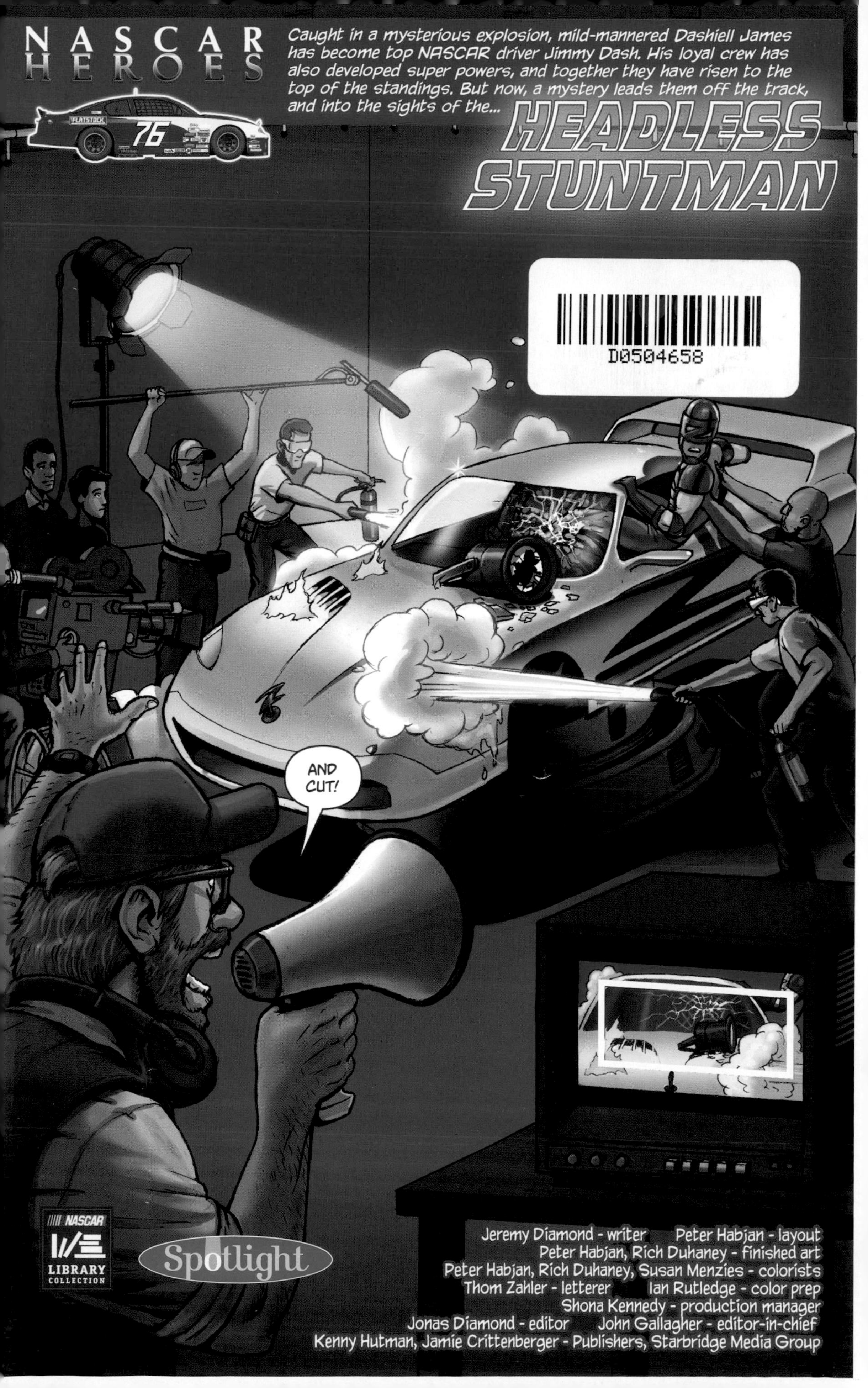
NASCAR HEROES
Caught in a mysterious explosion, mild-mannered Dashiell James has become top NASCAR driver Jimmy Dash. His loyal crew has also developed super powers, and together they have risen to the top of the standings. But now, a mystery leads them off the track, and into the sights of the...
HEADLESS STUNTMAN
AND CUT!
NASCAR
LIBRARY COLLECTION
Spotlight

Jeremy Diamond - writer Peter Habjan - layout
Peter Habjan, Rich Duhaney - finished art
Peter Habjan, Rich Duhaney, Susan Menzies - colorists
Thom Zahler - letterer Ian Rutledge - color prep
Shona Kennedy - production manager
Jonas Diamond - editor John Gallagher - editor-in-chief
Kenny Hutman, Jamie Crittenberger - Publishers, Starbridge Media Group

VISIT US AT
www.abdopublishing.com

Reinforced library bound edition published in 2010 by Spotlight, a division of the ABDO Group, 8000 West 78th Street, Edina, Minnesota 55439. Spotlight produces high-quality reinforced library bound editions for schools and libraries. Published by agreement with Starbridge Media Group, Inc.

Library of Congress Cataloging-in-Publication Data

Diamond, Jeremy.
  Headless stuntman / Jeremy Diamond, writer ; Peter Habjan, Rich Duhaney, finished art. --
Reinforced library bound ed.
     p. cm. -- (NASCAR heroes ; #4)
  "Nascar Library Collection."
  Summary: During the off-season, superhero NASCAR driver Jimmy Dash skips practice to take over the lead role in a racing movie, unaware that the set is haunted by a stuntman determined to stop the filming.
  ISBN 978-1-59961-665-0
  1. Graphic novels. [1. Graphic novels. 2. Automobile racing--Fiction. 3. NASCAR (Association)--Fiction. 4. Superheroes--Fiction. 5. Motion pictures--Production and direction--Fiction. 6. Ghosts--Fiction.] I. Habjan, Peter, ill. II. Duhaney, Rich, ill. III. Title.
  PZ7.7.D52Hec 2009
  741.5'973--dc22

                           2009009010

All Spotlight books have reinforced library bindings and
are manufactured in the United States of

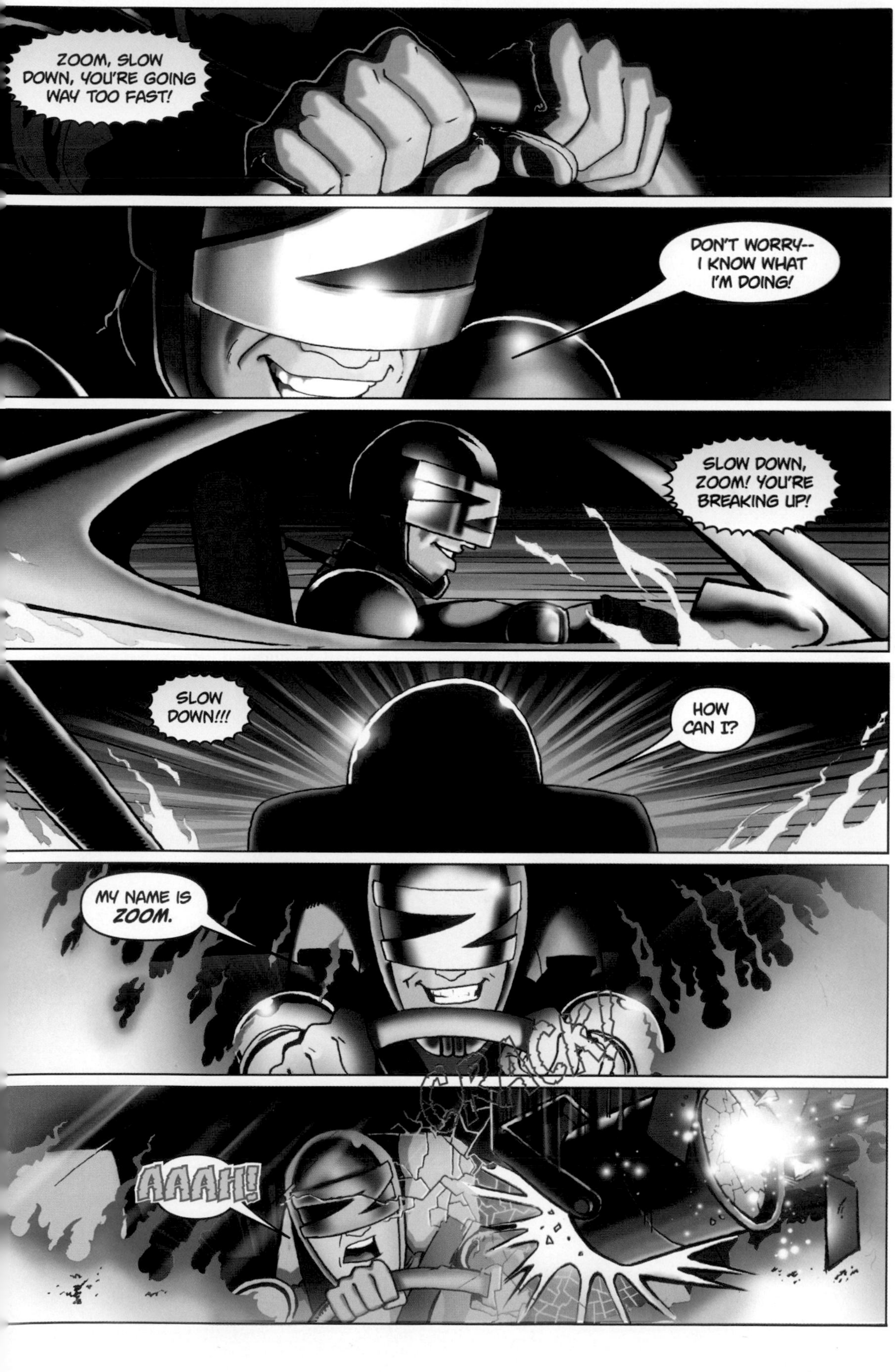
ZOOM, SLOW DOWN, YOU'RE GOING WAY TOO FAST!
DON'T WORRY-- I KNOW WHAT I'M DOING!
SLOW DOWN, ZOOM! YOU'RE BREAKING UP!
SLOW DOWN!!!
HOW CAN I?
MY NAME IS ZOOM.
AAAH!

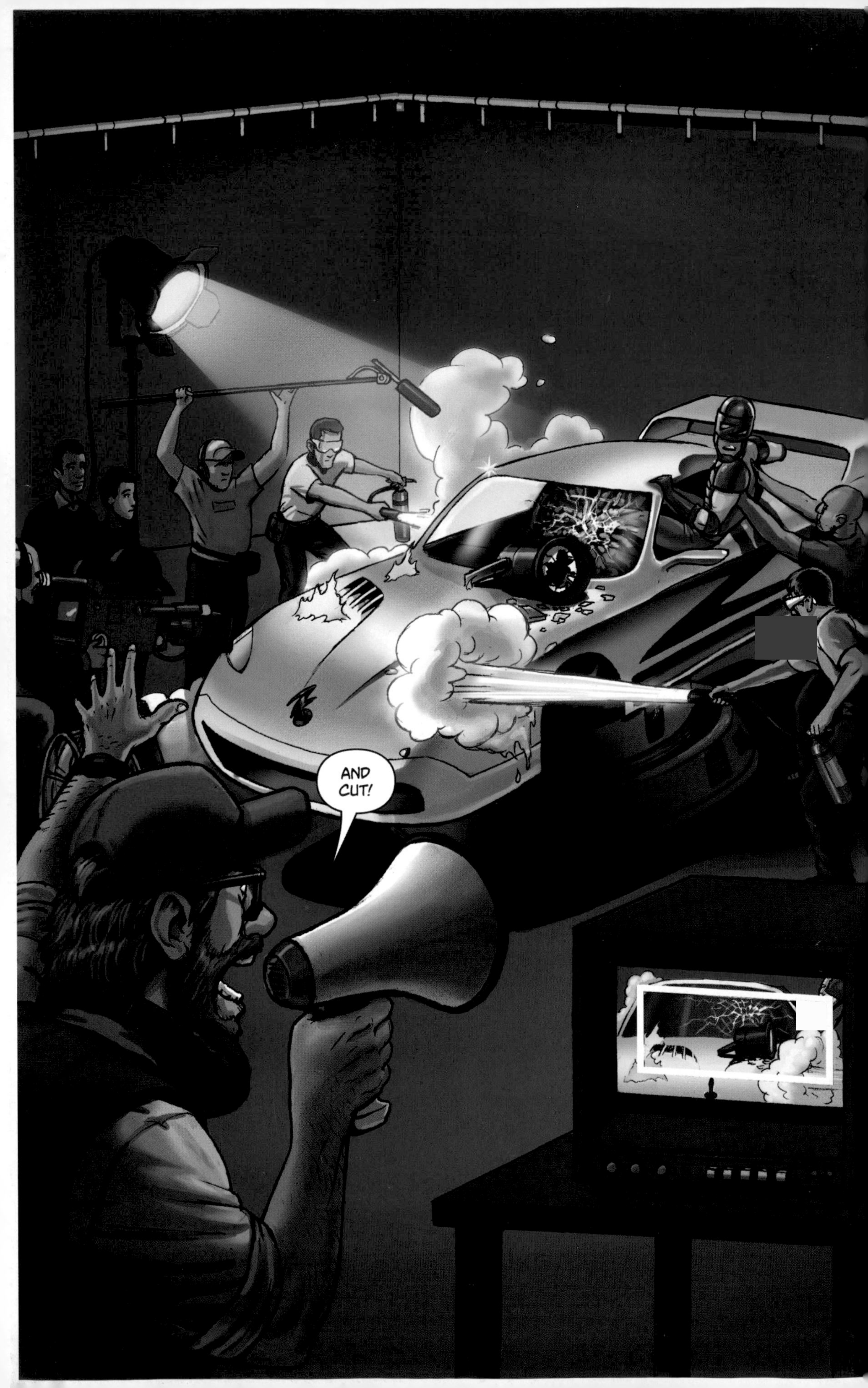
AND CUT!

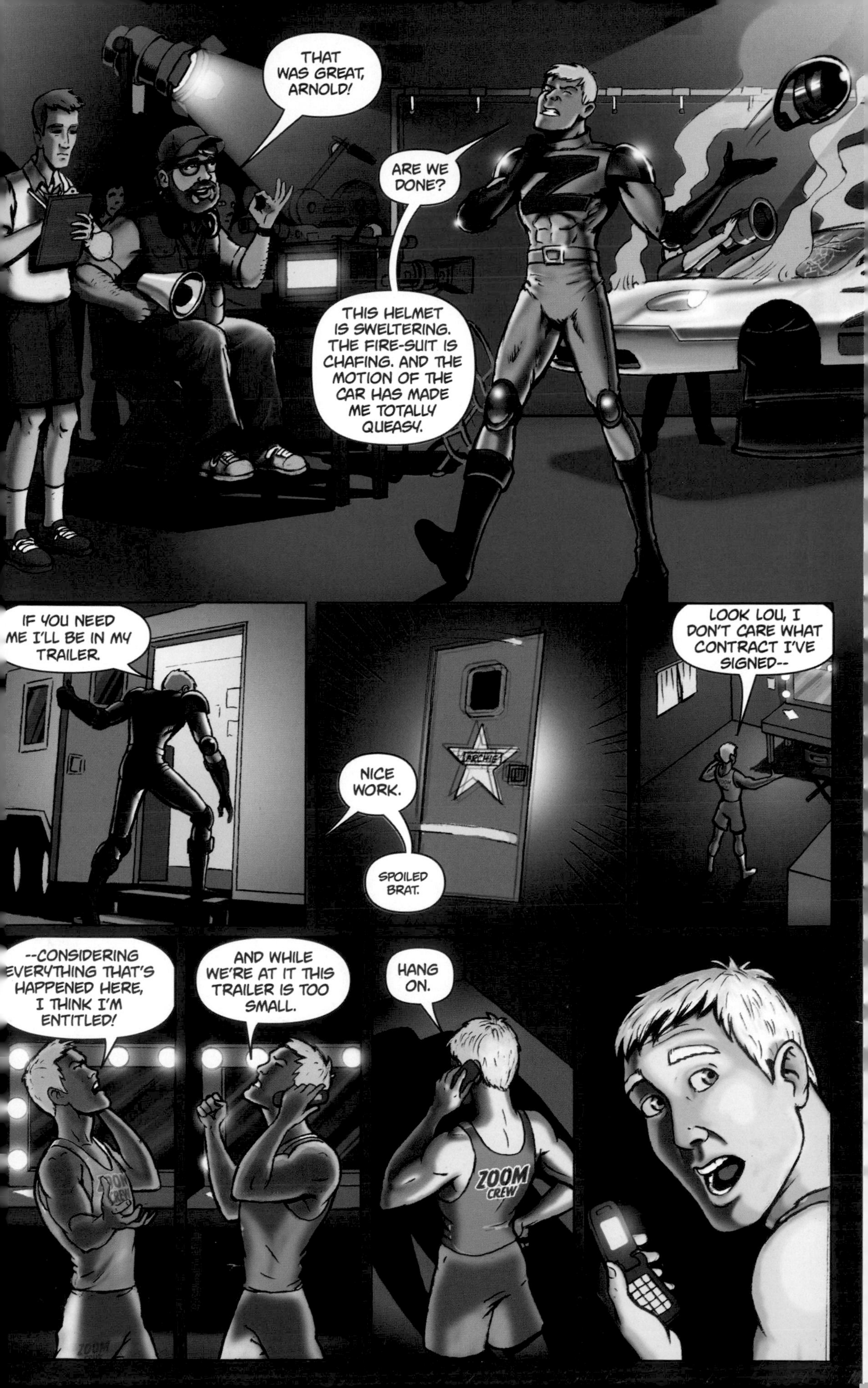
THAT WAS GREAT, ARNOLD!
ARE WE DONE?
THIS HELMET IS SWELTERING. THE FIRE-SUIT IS CHAFING. AND THE MOTION OF THE CAR HAS MADE ME TOTALLY QUEASY.
IF YOU NEED ME I'LL BE IN MY TRAILER.
ARCHIE
NICE WORK.
SPOILED BRAT.
LOOK LOU, I DON'T CARE WHAT CONTRACT I'VE SIGNED--
--CONSIDERING EVERYTHING THAT'S HAPPENED HERE, I THINK I'M ENTITLED!
AND WHILE WE'RE AT IT THIS TRAILER IS TOO SMALL.
HANG ON.
ZOOM CREW

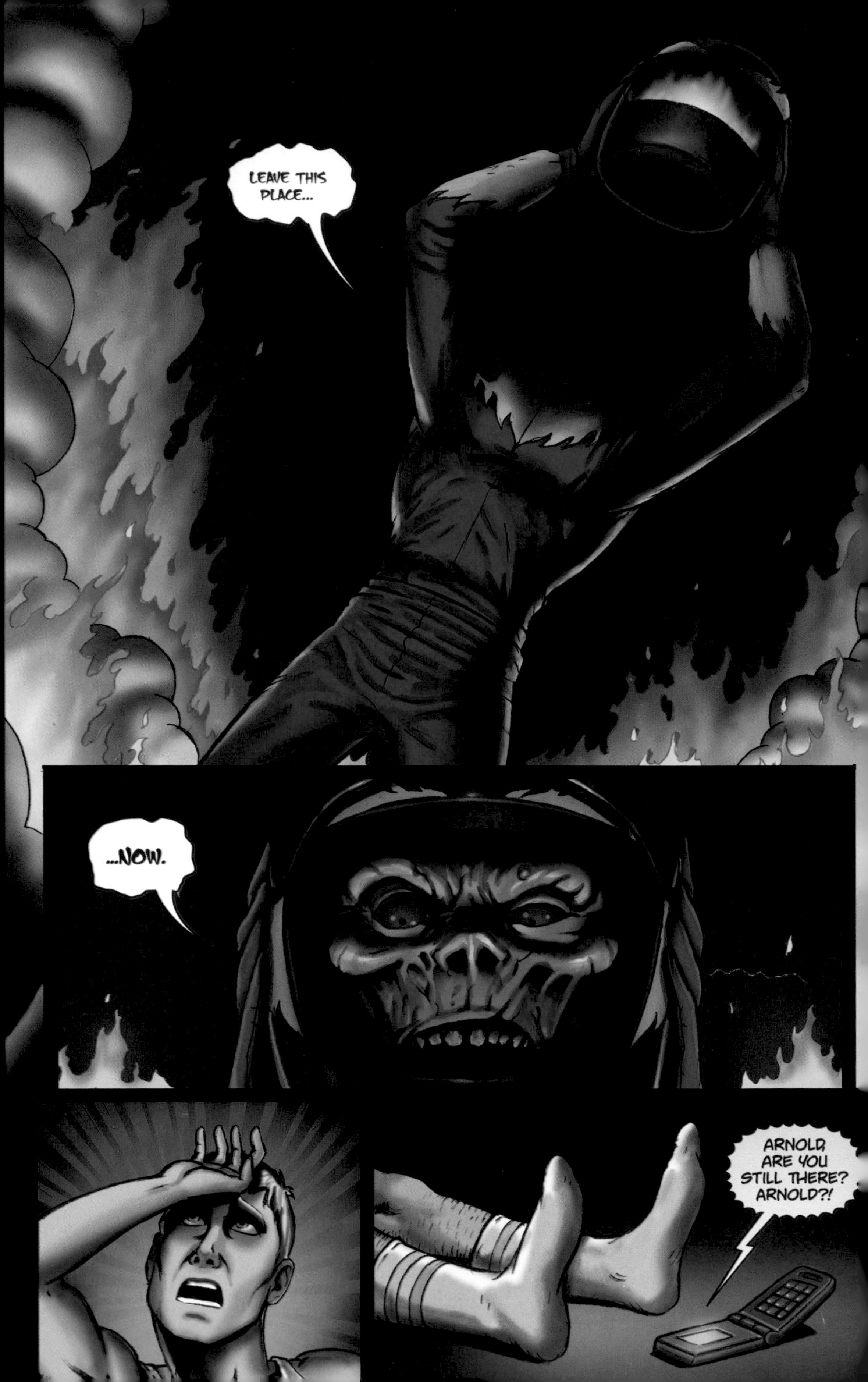
LEAVE THIS PLACE...
...NOW.
ARNOLD, ARE YOU STILL THERE? ARNOLD?!

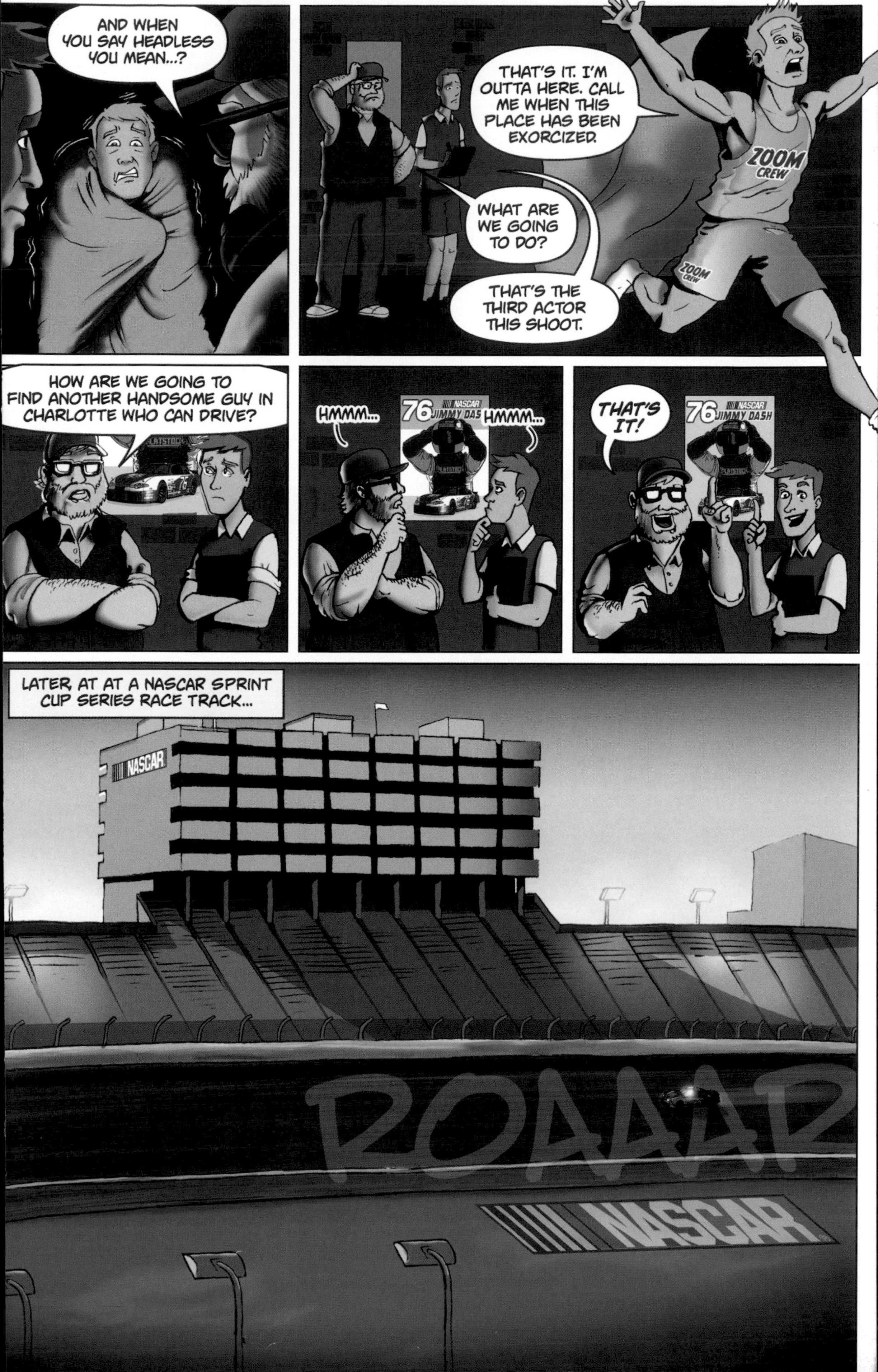
AND WHEN YOU SAY HEADLESS YOU MEAN...?
THAT'S IT. I'M OUTTA HERE. CALL ME WHEN THIS PLACE HAS BEEN EXORCIZED.
ZOOM CREW
WHAT ARE WE GOING TO DO?
THAT'S THE THIRD ACTOR THIS SHOOT.
HOW ARE WE GOING TO FIND ANOTHER HANDSOME GUY IN CHARLOTTE WHO CAN DRIVE?
HMMM...
76 NASCAR JIMMY DAS
HMMM...
THAT'S IT!
76 NASCAR JIMMY DASH
LATER, AT AT A NASCAR SPRINT CUP SERIES RACE TRACK...
NASCAR
ROAAAR
NASCAR

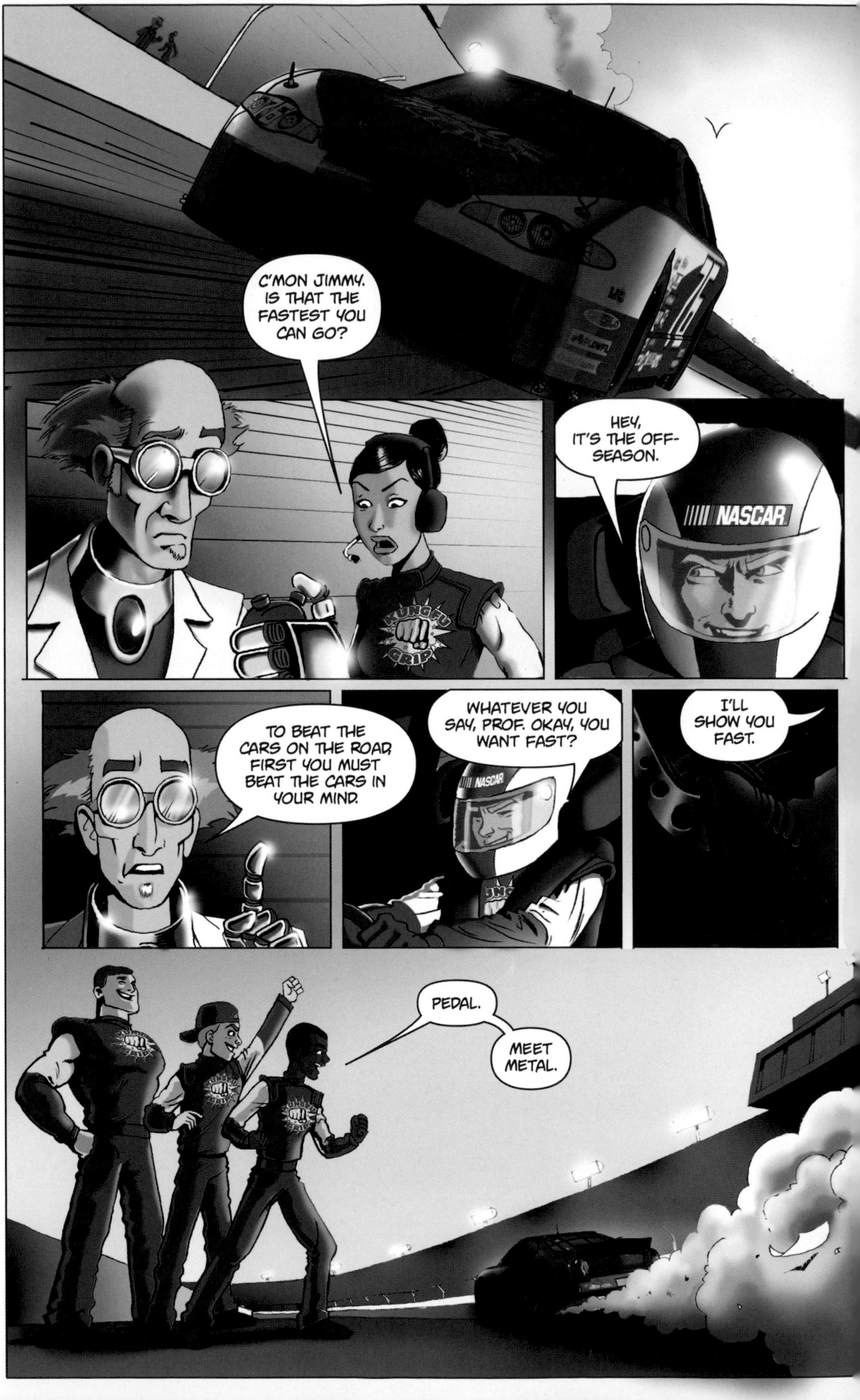
C'MON JIMMY. IS THAT THE FASTEST YOU CAN GO?
HEY, IT'S THE OFF-SEASON.
NASCAR
TO BEAT THE CARS ON THE ROAD, FIRST YOU MUST BEAT THE CARS IN YOUR MIND.
WHATEVER YOU SAY, PROF. OKAY, YOU WANT FAST?
I'LL SHOW YOU FAST.
PEDAL.
MEET METAL.

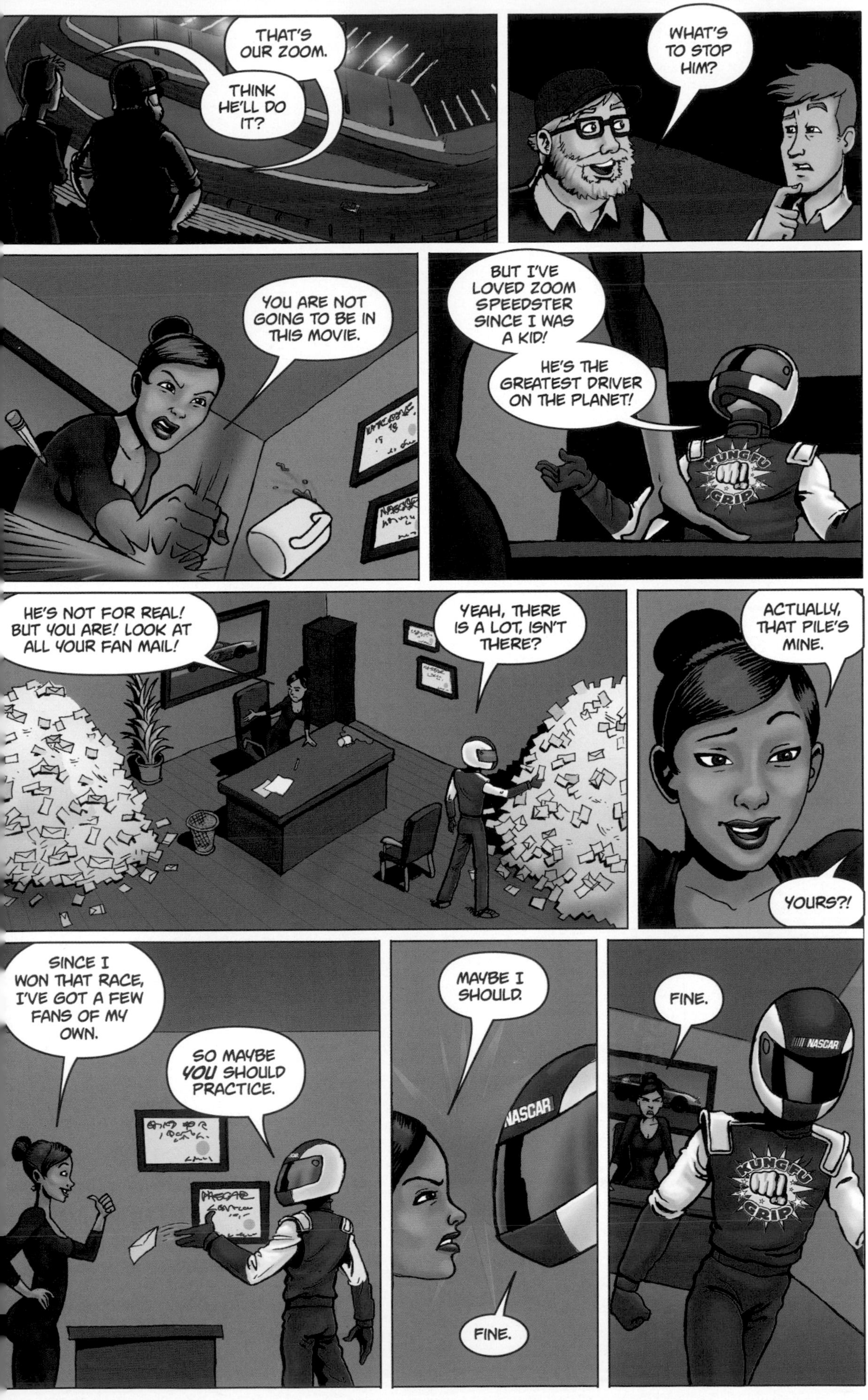
THAT'S OUR ZOOM.
THINK HE'LL DO IT?
WHAT'S TO STOP HIM?
YOU ARE NOT GOING TO BE IN THIS MOVIE.
BUT I'VE LOVED ZOOM SPEEDSTER SINCE I WAS A KID!
HE'S THE GREATEST DRIVER ON THE PLANET!
KUNG FU GRIP
HE'S NOT FOR REAL! BUT YOU ARE! LOOK AT ALL YOUR FAN MAIL!
YEAH, THERE IS A LOT, ISN'T THERE?
ACTUALLY, THAT PILE'S MINE.
YOURS?!
SINCE I WON THAT RACE, I'VE GOT A FEW FANS OF MY OWN.
SO MAYBE *YOU* SHOULD PRACTICE.
MAYBE I SHOULD.
NASCAR
FINE.
FINE.
NASCAR
KUNG FU GRIP

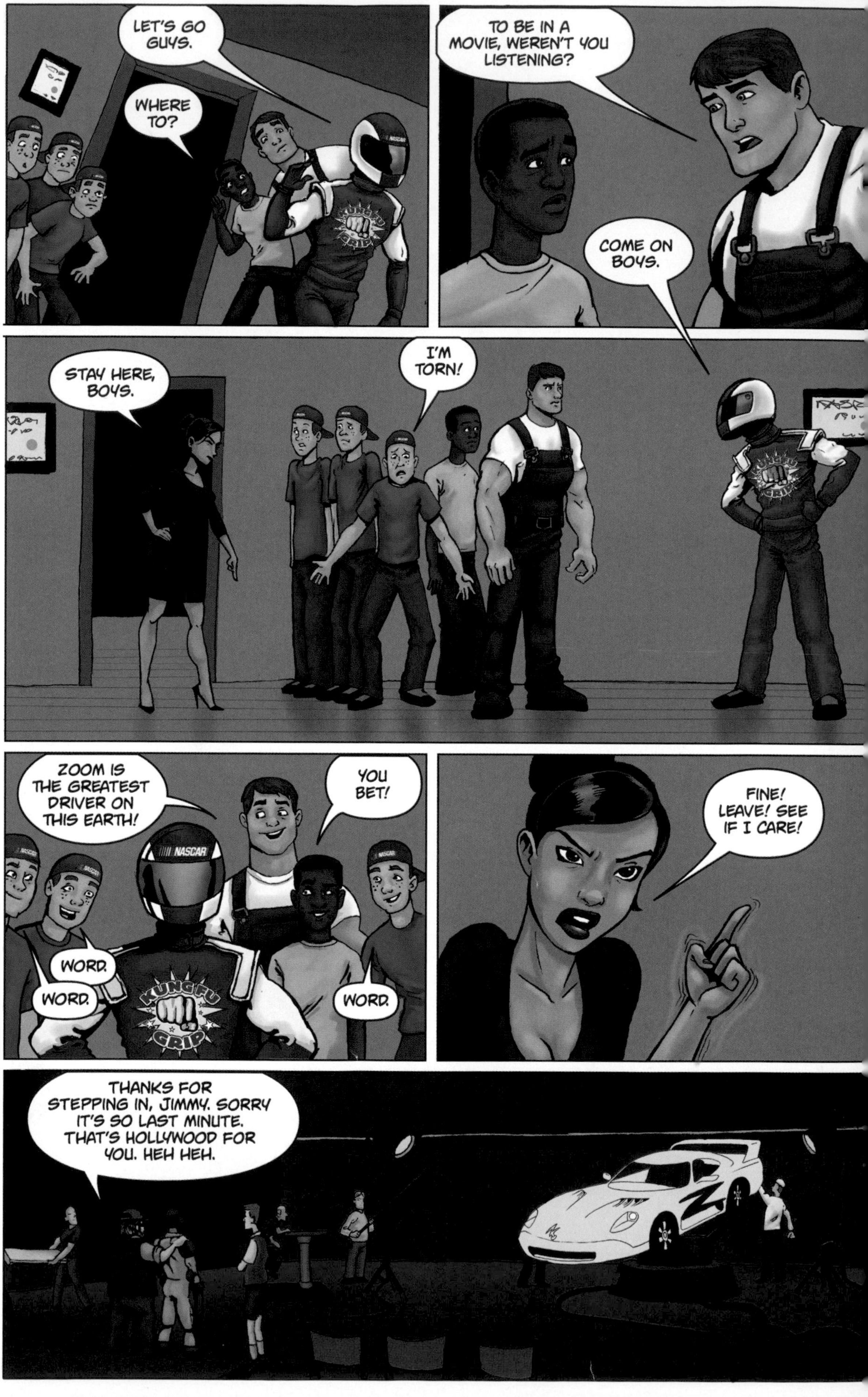
LET'S GO GUYS.
WHERE TO?
TO BE IN A MOVIE, WEREN'T YOU LISTENING?
COME ON BOYS.
STAY HERE, BOYS.
I'M TORN!
ZOOM IS THE GREATEST DRIVER ON THIS EARTH!
YOU BET!
WORD.
WORD.
WORD.
FINE! LEAVE! SEE IF I CARE!
THANKS FOR STEPPING IN, JIMMY. SORRY IT'S SO LAST MINUTE. THAT'S HOLLYWOOD FOR YOU. HEH HEH.

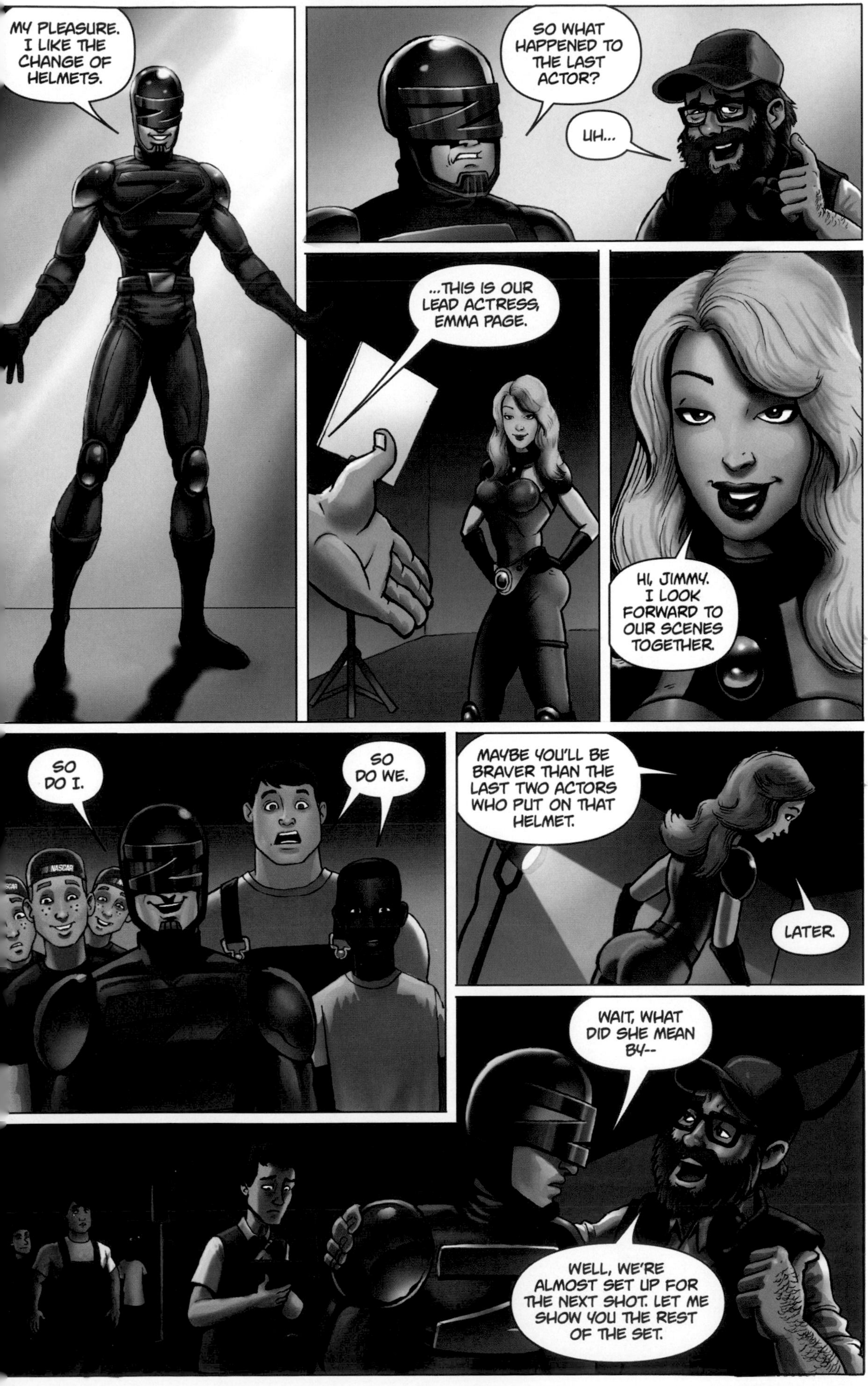
MY PLEASURE. I LIKE THE CHANGE OF HELMETS.
SO WHAT HAPPENED TO THE LAST ACTOR?
UH...
...THIS IS OUR LEAD ACTRESS, EMMA PAGE.
HI, JIMMY. I LOOK FORWARD TO OUR SCENES TOGETHER.
SO DO I.
SO DO WE.
NASCAR
MAYBE YOU'LL BE BRAVER THAN THE LAST TWO ACTORS WHO PUT ON THAT HELMET.
LATER.
WAIT, WHAT DID SHE MEAN BY--
WELL, WE'RE ALMOST SET UP FOR THE NEXT SHOT. LET ME SHOW YOU THE REST OF THE SET.

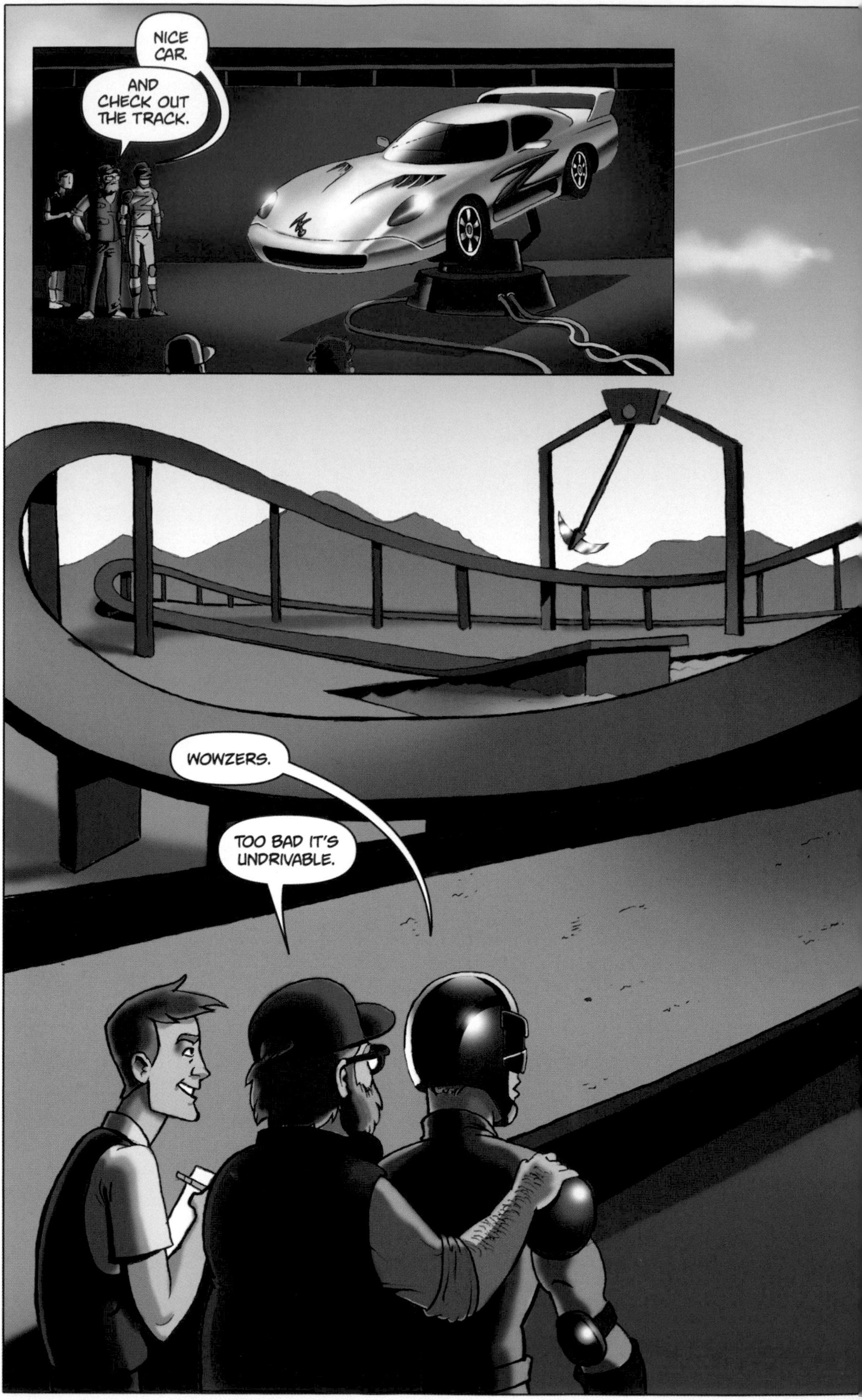
NICE CAR.
AND CHECK OUT THE TRACK.
WOWZERS.
TOO BAD IT'S UNDRIVABLE.

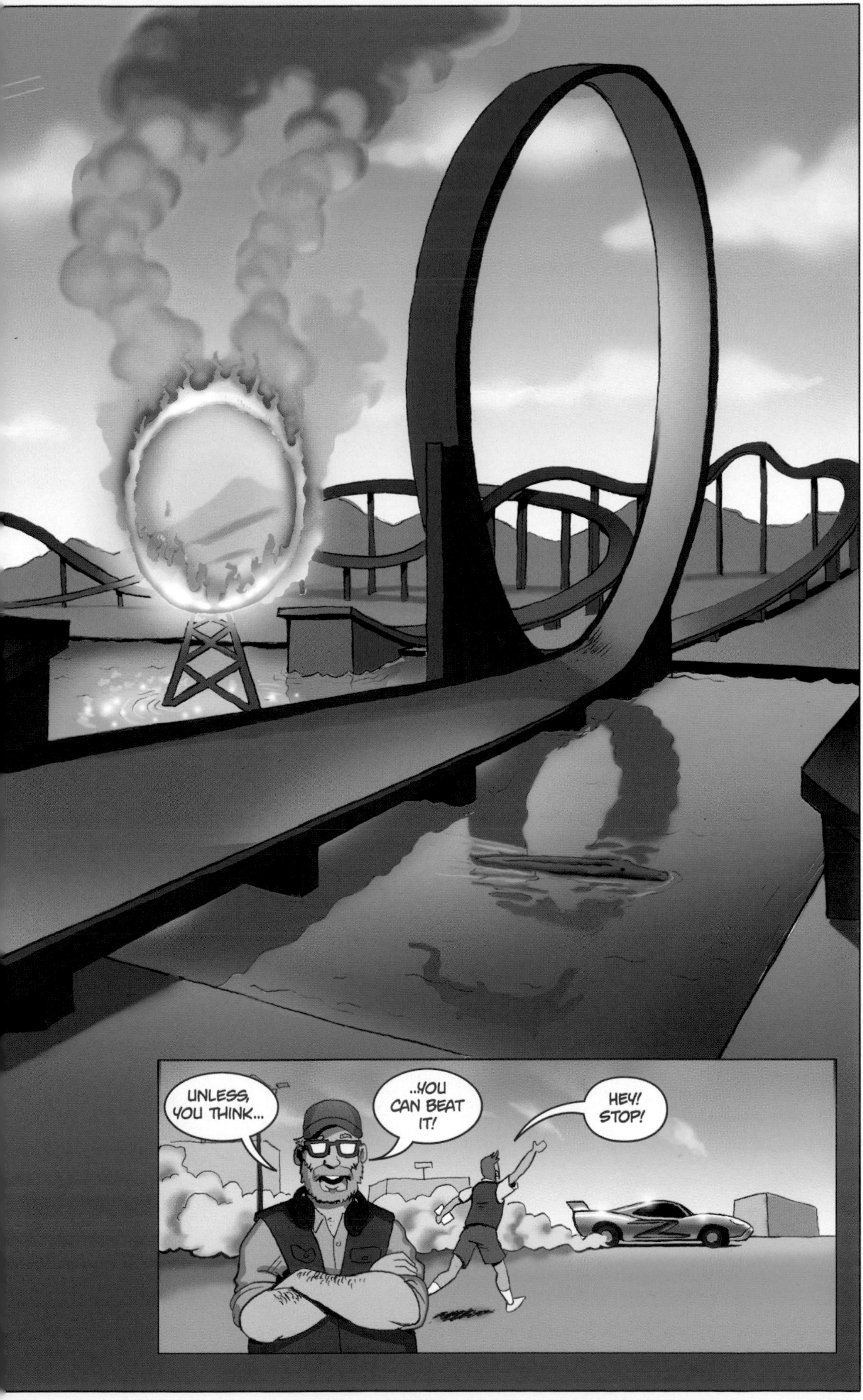
UNLESS, YOU THINK...
..YOU CAN BEAT IT!
HEY! STOP!

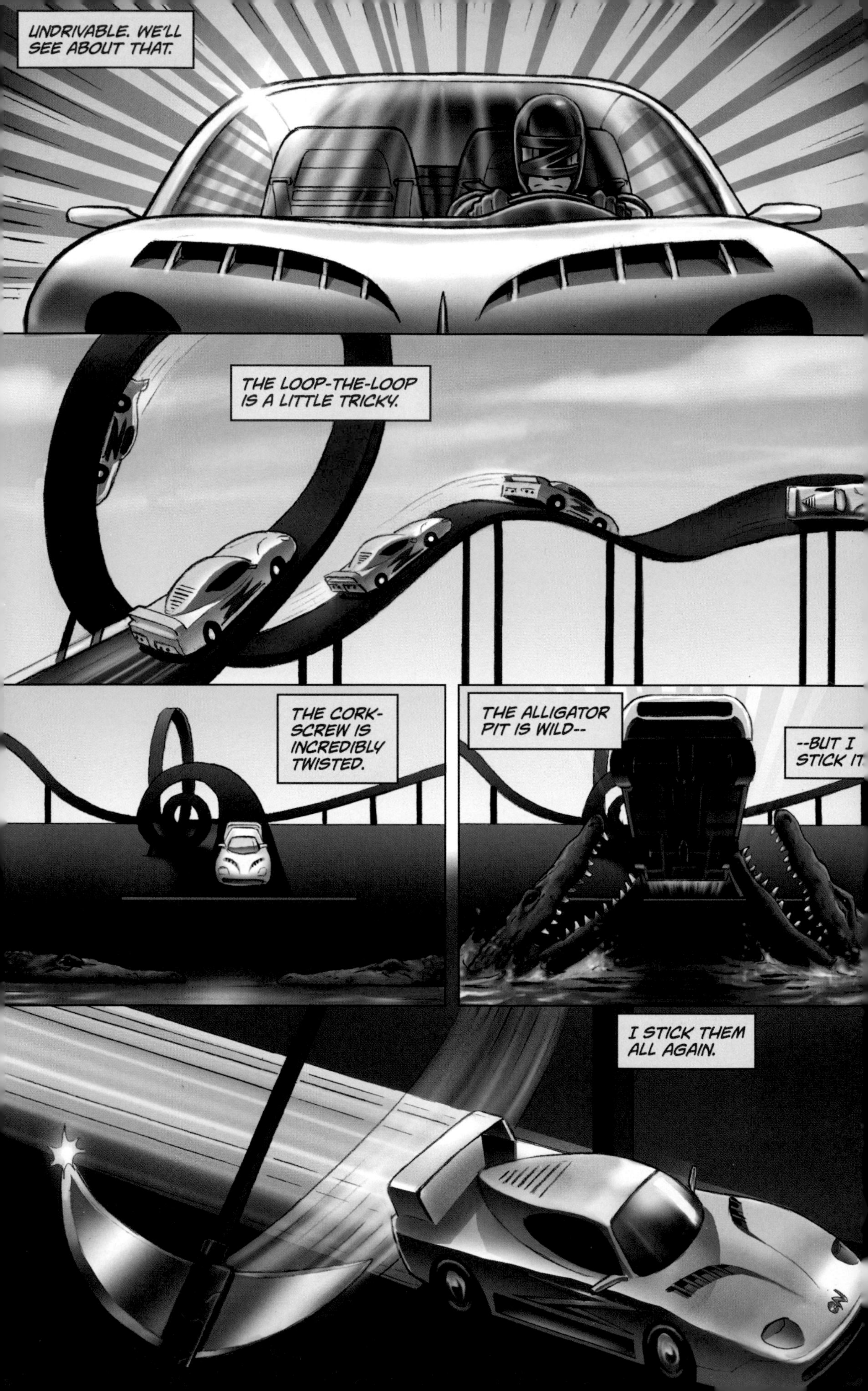
UNDRIVABLE. WE'LL SEE ABOUT THAT.
THE LOOP-THE-LOOP IS A LITTLE TRICKY.
THE CORK-SCREW IS INCREDIBLY TWISTED.
THE ALLIGATOR PIT IS WILD--
--BUT I STICK IT.
I STICK THEM ALL AGAIN.

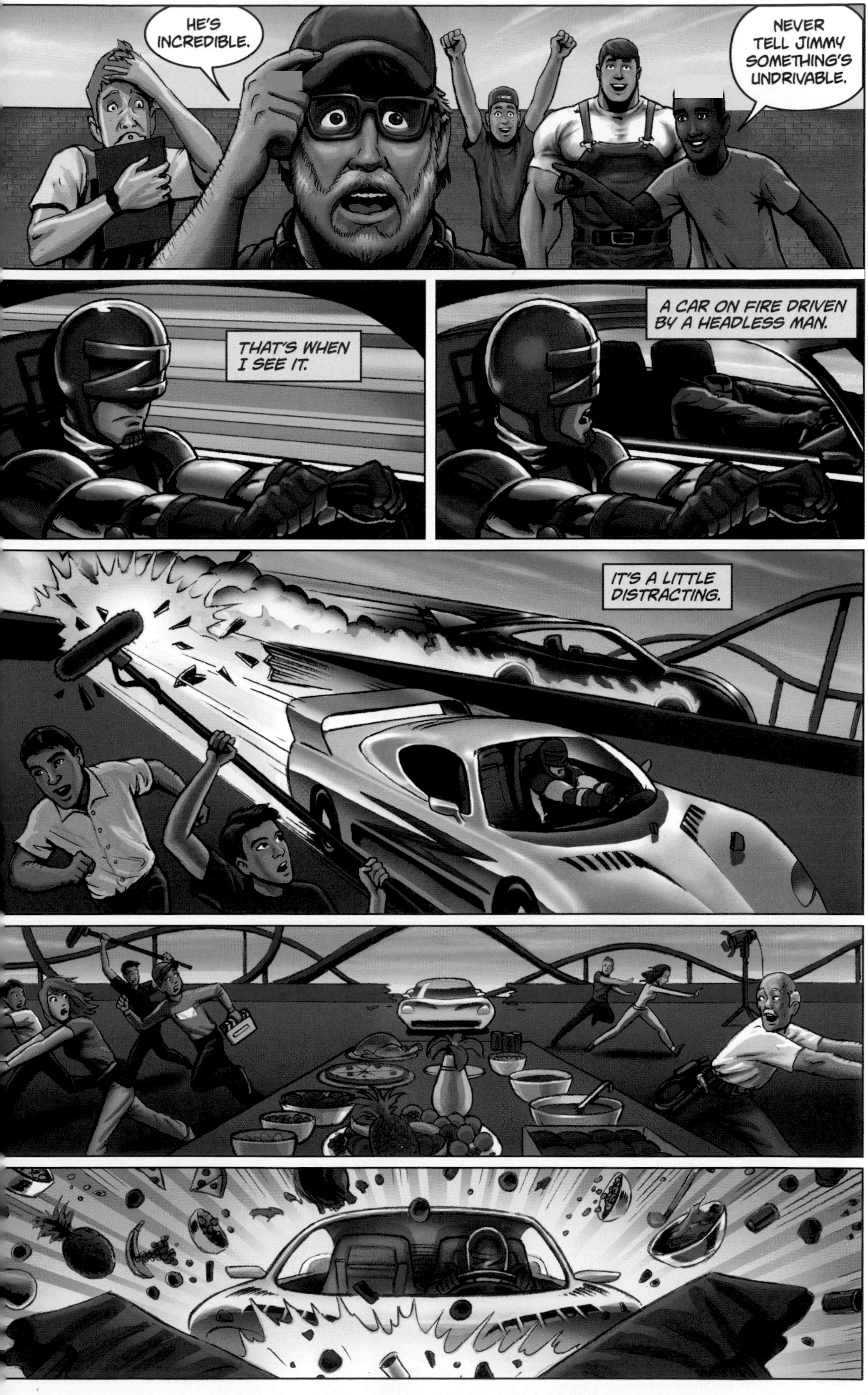
HE'S INCREDIBLE.
NEVER TELL JIMMY SOMETHING'S UNDRIVABLE.
THAT'S WHEN I SEE IT.
A CAR ON FIRE DRIVEN BY A HEADLESS MAN.
IT'S A LITTLE DISTRACTING.

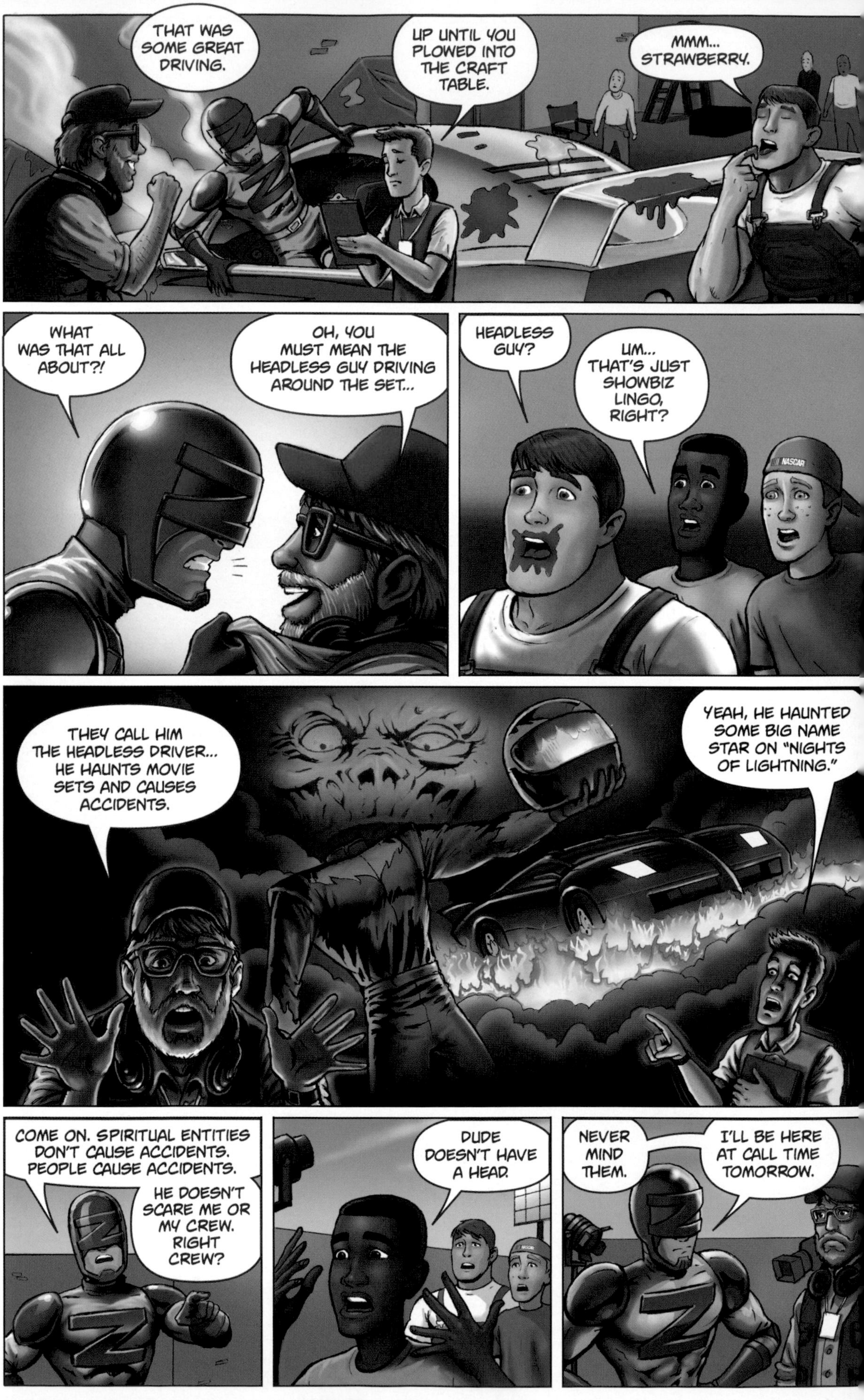
THAT WAS SOME GREAT DRIVING.
UP UNTIL YOU PLOWED INTO THE CRAFT TABLE.
MMM... STRAWBERRY.
WHAT WAS THAT ALL ABOUT?!
OH, YOU MUST MEAN THE HEADLESS GUY DRIVING AROUND THE SET...
HEADLESS GUY?
UM... THAT'S JUST SHOWBIZ LINGO, RIGHT?
NASCAR
THEY CALL HIM THE HEADLESS DRIVER... HE HAUNTS MOVIE SETS AND CAUSES ACCIDENTS.
YEAH, HE HAUNTED SOME BIG NAME STAR ON "NIGHTS OF LIGHTNING."
COME ON. SPIRITUAL ENTITIES DON'T CAUSE ACCIDENTS. PEOPLE CAUSE ACCIDENTS.
HE DOESN'T SCARE ME OR MY CREW. RIGHT CREW?
DUDE DOESN'T HAVE A HEAD.
NEVER MIND THEM.
I'LL BE HERE AT CALL TIME TOMORROW.

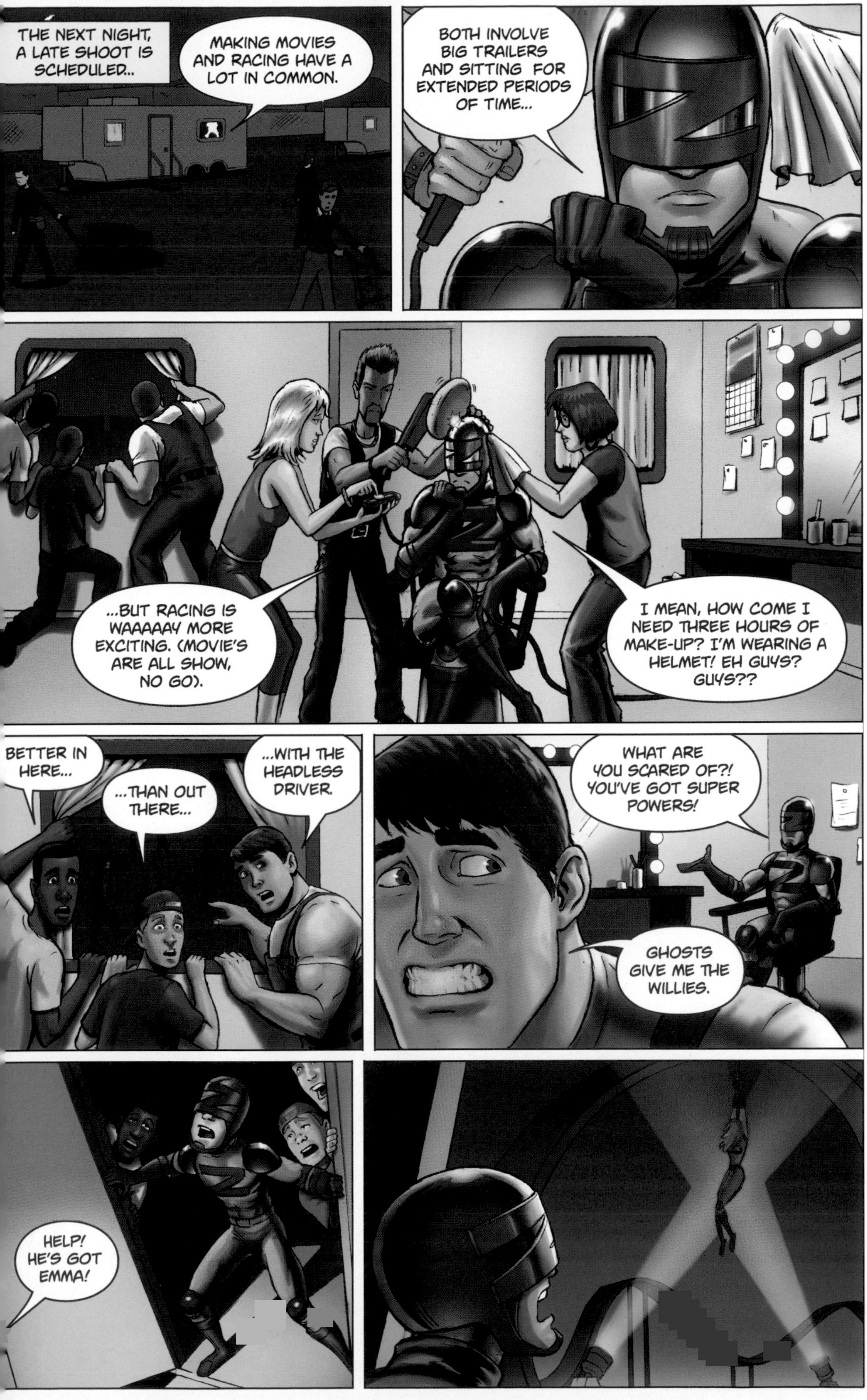
THE NEXT NIGHT, A LATE SHOOT IS SCHEDULED...
MAKING MOVIES AND RACING HAVE A LOT IN COMMON.
BOTH INVOLVE BIG TRAILERS AND SITTING FOR EXTENDED PERIODS OF TIME...
...BUT RACING IS WAAAAAY MORE EXCITING. (MOVIE'S ARE ALL SHOW, NO GO).
I MEAN, HOW COME I NEED THREE HOURS OF MAKE-UP? I'M WEARING A HELMET! EH GUYS? GUYS??
BETTER IN HERE...
...THAN OUT THERE...
...WITH THE HEADLESS DRIVER.
WHAT ARE YOU SCARED OF?! YOU'VE GOT SUPER POWERS!
GHOSTS GIVE ME THE WILLIES.
HELP! HE'S GOT EMMA!

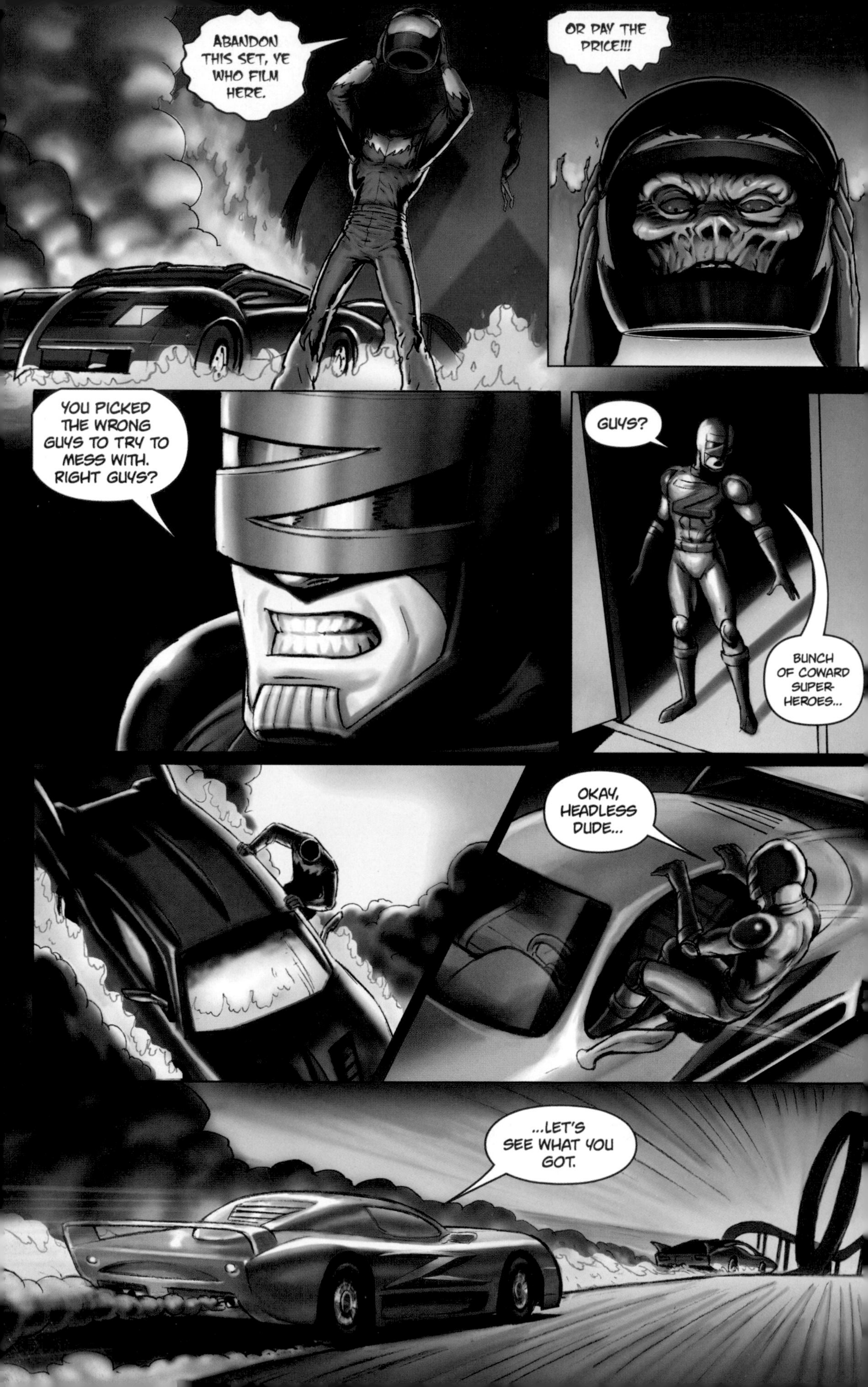
ABANDON THIS SET, YE WHO FILM HERE.
OR PAY THE PRICE!!!
YOU PICKED THE WRONG GUYS TO TRY TO MESS WITH. RIGHT GUYS?
GUYS?
BUNCH OF COWARD SUPER-HEROES...
OKAY, HEADLESS DUDE...
...LET'S SEE WHAT YOU GOT.

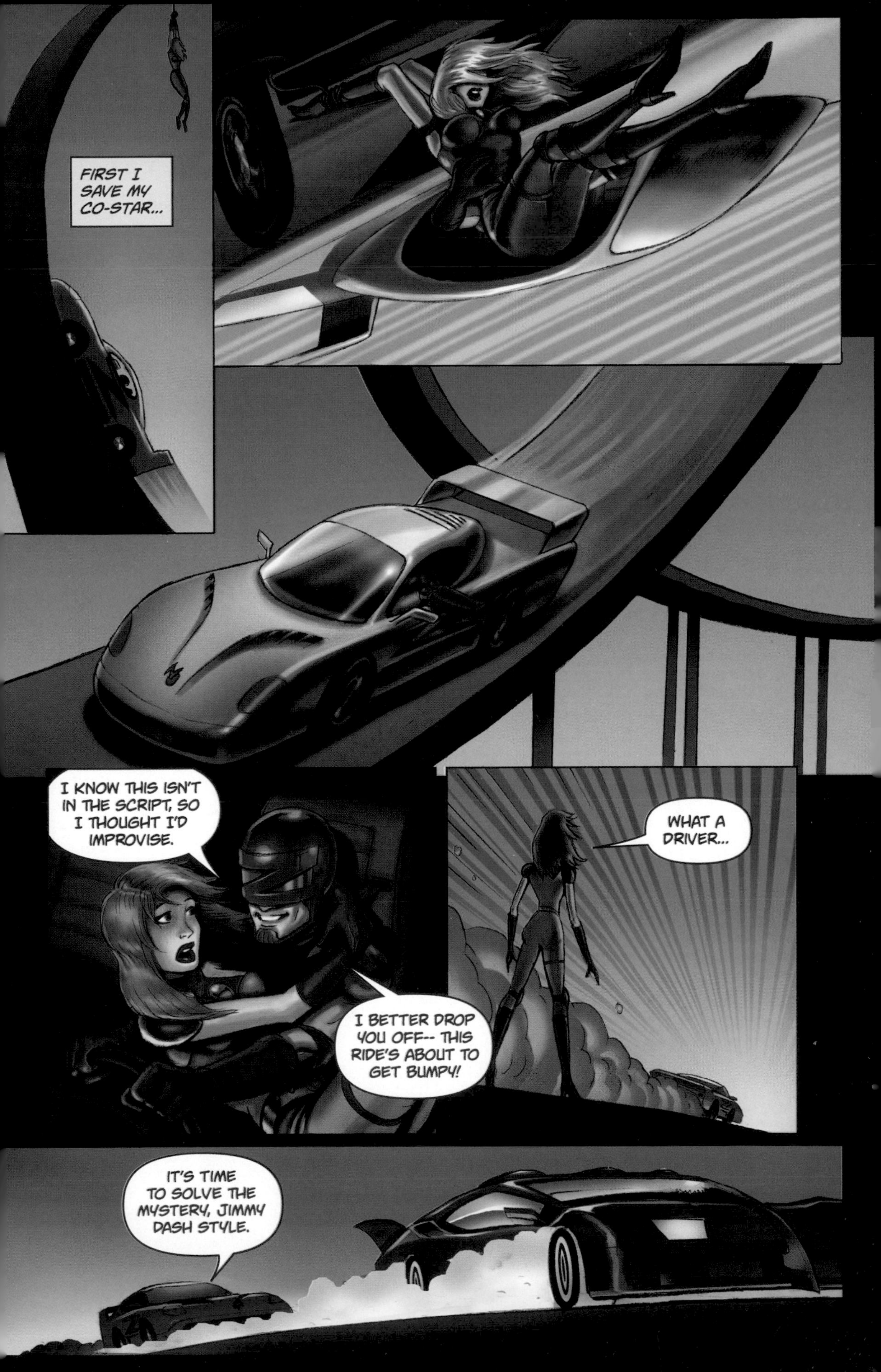
FIRST I SAVE MY CO-STAR...
I KNOW THIS ISN'T IN THE SCRIPT, SO I THOUGHT I'D IMPROVISE.
I BETTER DROP YOU OFF-- THIS RIDE'S ABOUT TO GET BUMPY!
WHAT A DRIVER...
IT'S TIME TO SOLVE THE MYSTERY, JIMMY DASH STYLE.

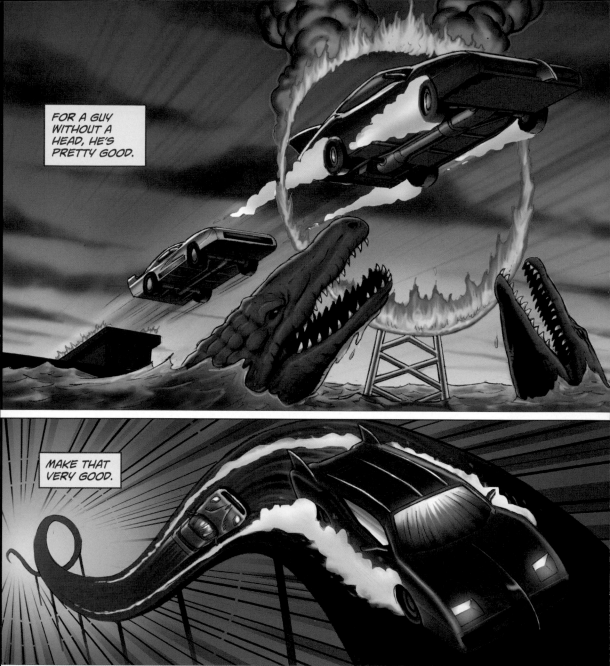

FOR A GUY WITHOUT A HEAD, HE'S PRETTY GOOD.

MAKE THAT VERY GOOD.

HIS CAR FEELS SOLID ENOUGH.

ENOUGH IS ENOUGH. TIME TO SEE WHAT THIS GHOST IS REALLY MADE OF.

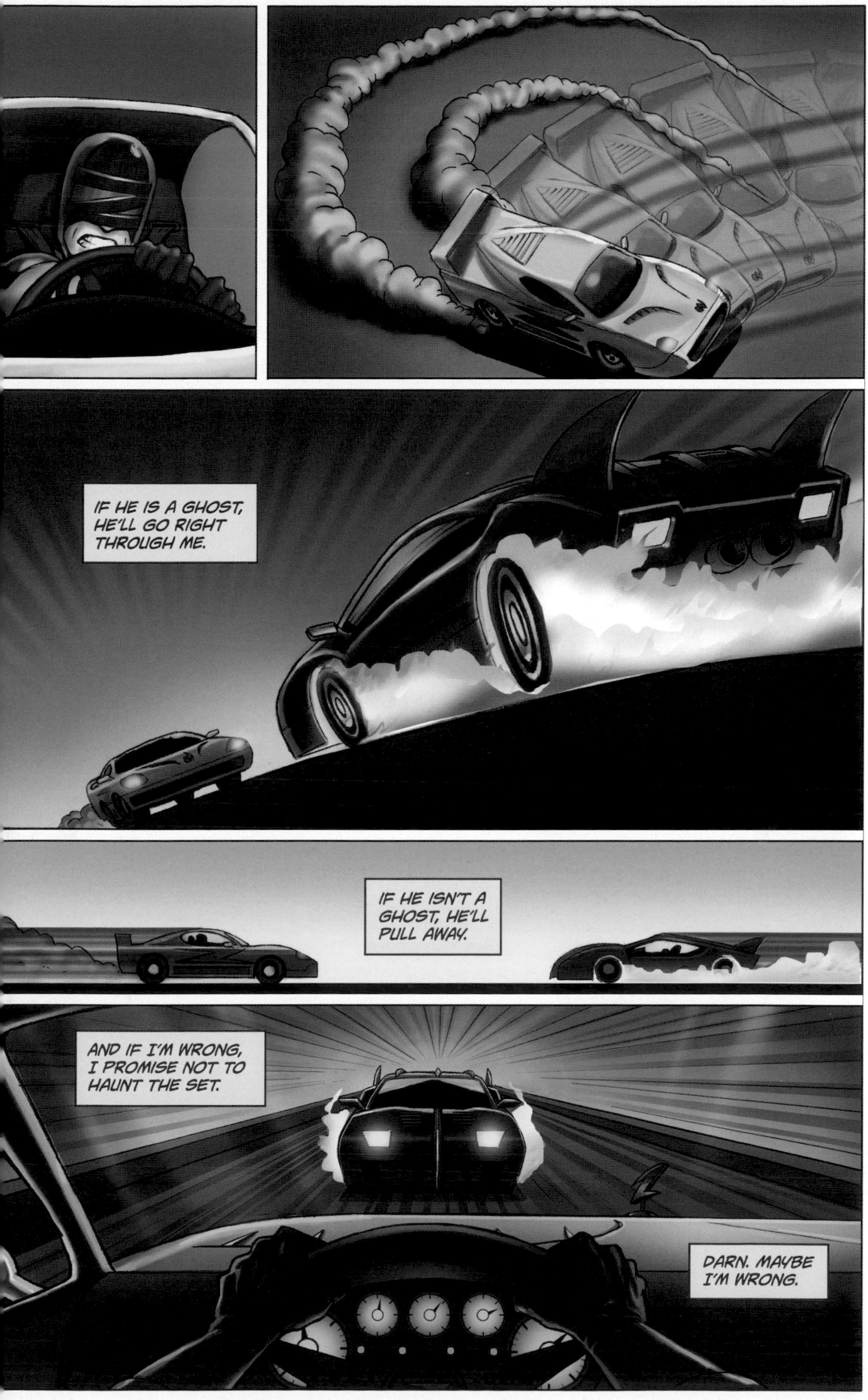
IF HE IS A GHOST, HE'LL GO RIGHT THROUGH ME.
IF HE ISN'T A GHOST, HE'LL PULL AWAY.
AND IF I'M WRONG, I PROMISE NOT TO HAUNT THE SET.
DARN. MAYBE I'M WRONG.

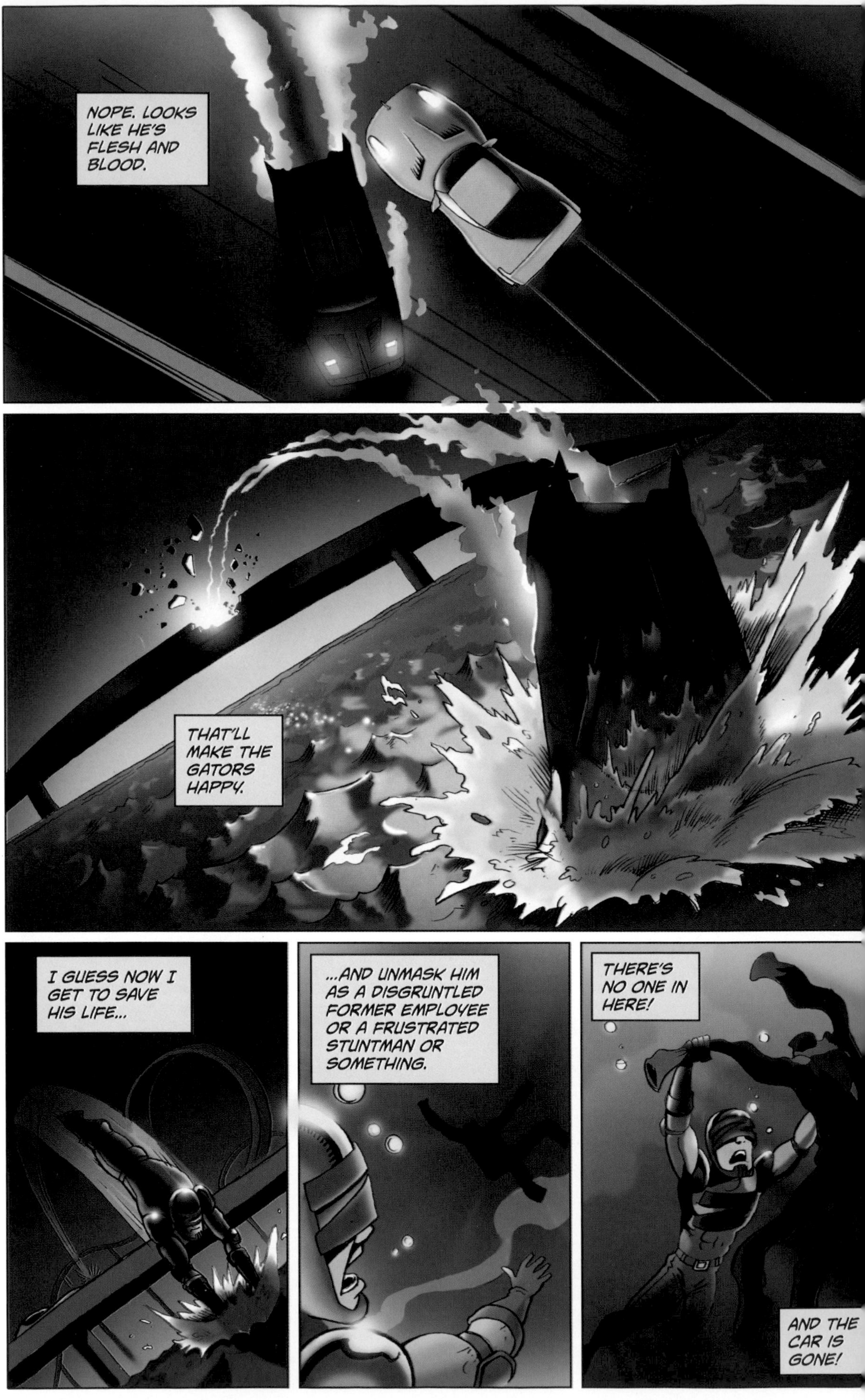
NOPE. LOOKS LIKE HE'S FLESH AND BLOOD.
THAT'LL MAKE THE GATORS HAPPY.
I GUESS NOW I GET TO SAVE HIS LIFE...
...AND UNMASK HIM AS A DISGRUNTLED FORMER EMPLOYEE OR A FRUSTRATED STUNTMAN OR SOMETHING.
THERE'S NO ONE IN HERE!
AND THE CAR IS GONE!

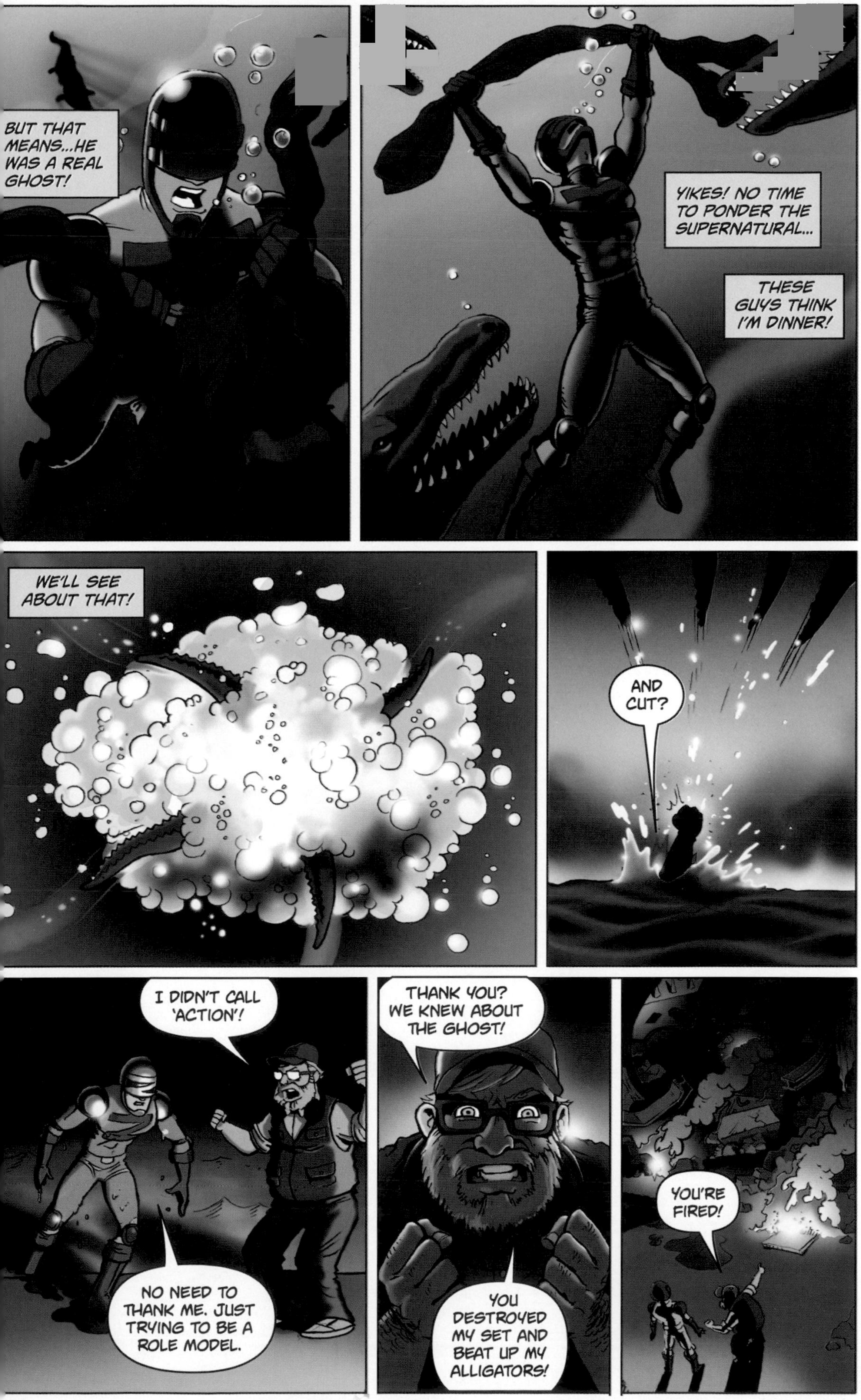
BUT THAT MEANS...HE WAS A REAL GHOST!
YIKES! NO TIME TO PONDER THE SUPERNATURAL...
THESE GUYS THINK I'M DINNER!
WE'LL SEE ABOUT THAT!
AND CUT?
I DIDN'T CALL 'ACTION'!
NO NEED TO THANK ME. JUST TRYING TO BE A ROLE MODEL.
THANK YOU? WE KNEW ABOUT THE GHOST!
YOU DESTROYED MY SET AND BEAT UP MY ALLIGATORS!
YOU'RE FIRED!

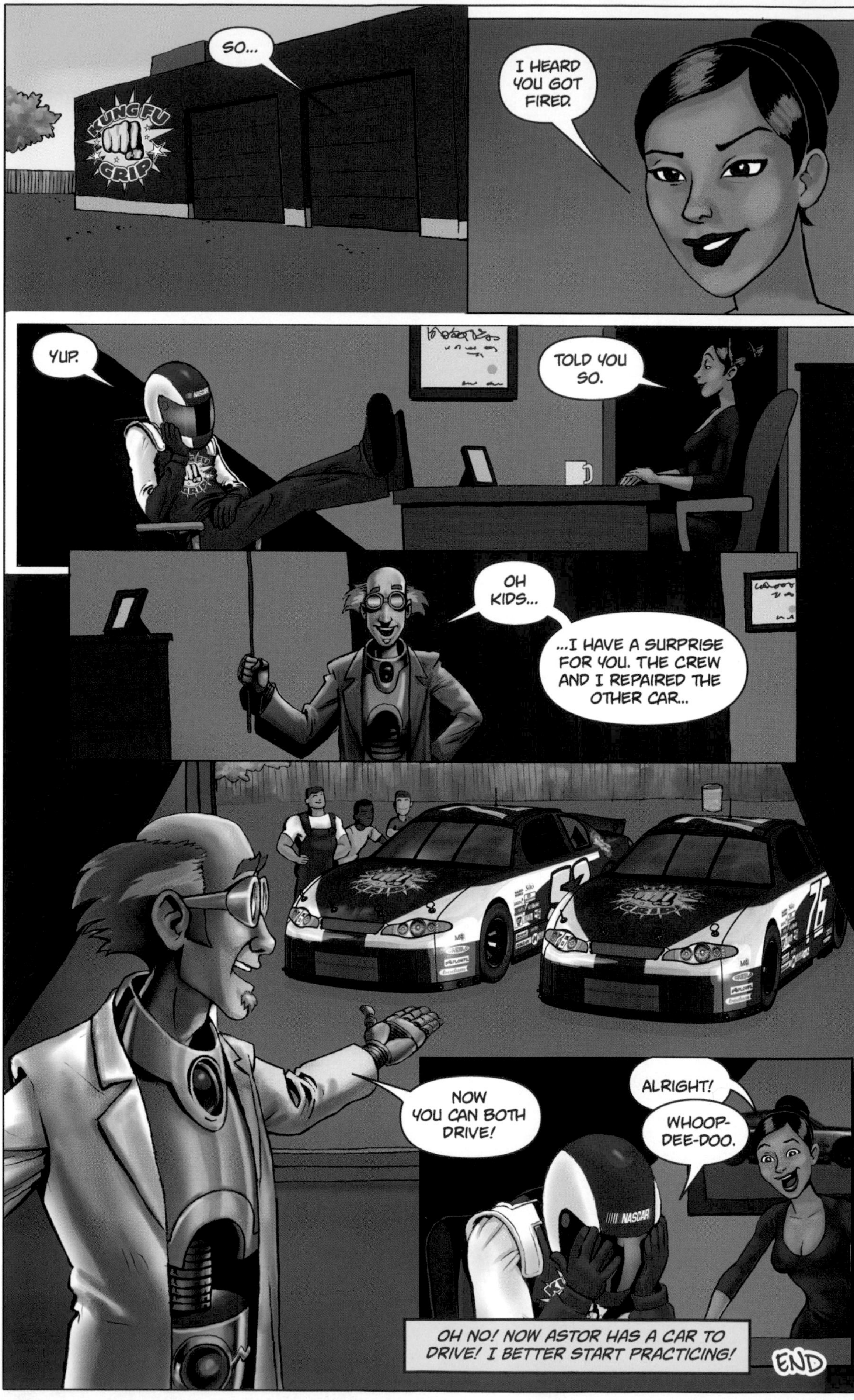
SO...
I HEARD YOU GOT FIRED.
YUP.
TOLD YOU SO.
OH KIDS...
...I HAVE A SURPRISE FOR YOU. THE CREW AND I REPAIRED THE OTHER CAR...
NOW YOU CAN BOTH DRIVE!
ALRIGHT!
WHOOP-DEE-DOO.
OH NO! NOW ASTOR HAS A CAR TO DRIVE! I BETTER START PRACTICING!
END

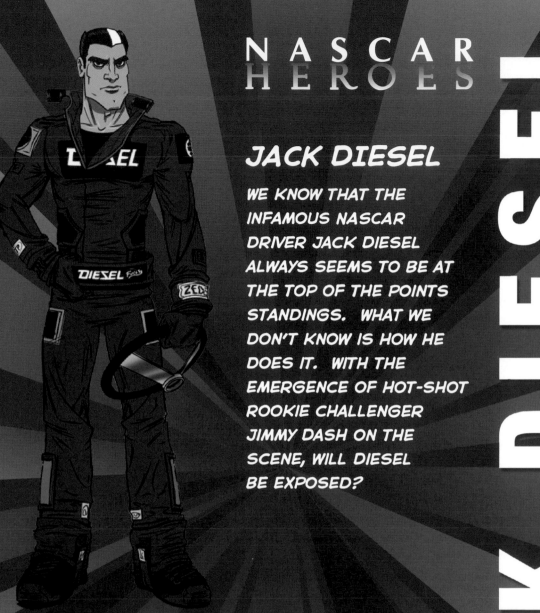

NASCAR HEROES

JACK DIESEL

DIESEL

JACK DIESEL

WE KNOW THAT THE INFAMOUS NASCAR DRIVER JACK DIESEL ALWAYS SEEMS TO BE AT THE TOP OF THE POINTS STANDINGS. WHAT WE DON'T KNOW IS HOW HE DOES IT. WITH THE EMERGENCE OF HOT-SHOT ROOKIE CHALLENGER JIMMY DASH ON THE SCENE, WILL DIESEL BE EXPOSED?

DIESEL INDUSTRIES
63

NASCAR HEROES

ASTOR SHOCKINGTON A.K.A SHOQUE

ASTOR SHOCKINGTON

AS THE OPERATIONS MANAGER OF NASCAR'S LOWLIEST RACING TEAM, FLATSTOCK, MS. ASTOR SHOCKINGTON IS FRUSTRATED BY HER BLUNDERING CREW. TRANSFORMED INTO SUPERHEROINE "SHOQUE," SHE USES HER SPECIAL POWERS TO HELP TEAM FLATSTOCK TOWARDS A TEAM CHAMPIONSHIP.

56
GREELO
PLOWFL
bodum

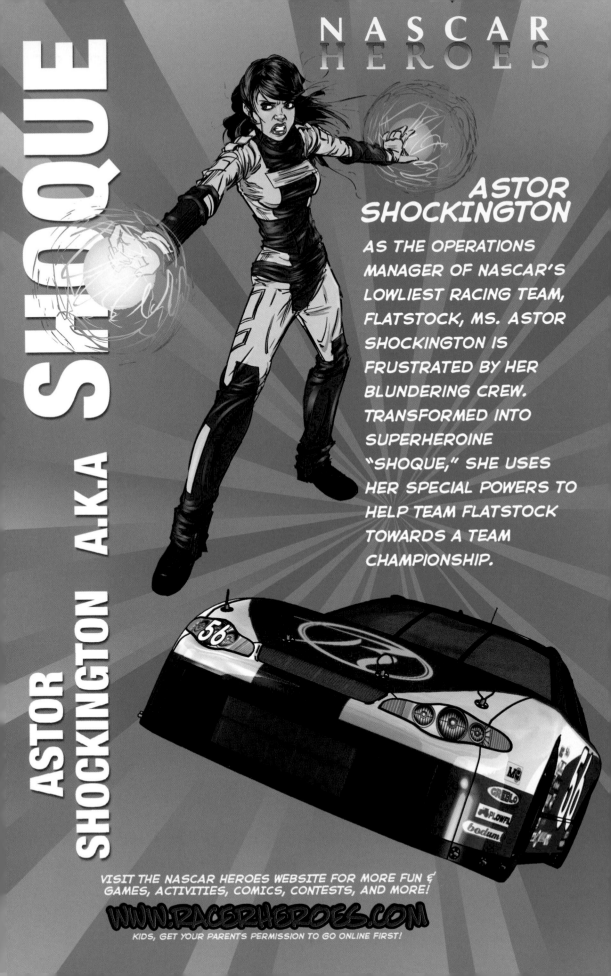

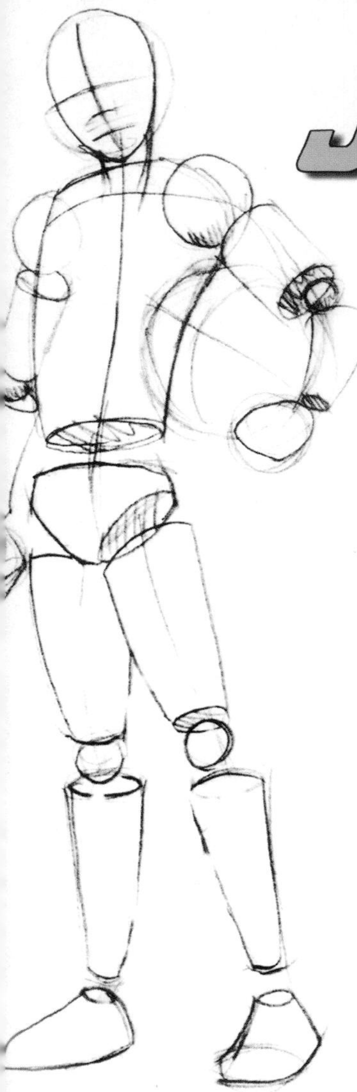

HOW TO DRAW JIMMY DASH

NASCAR COMICS

BY JOHN GALLAGHER

STEP 1: USING A PENCIL, BEGIN WITH A SIMPLE FRAMEWORK. A STICK FIGURE WILL DO THE TRICK TO START! ADD CIRCLES, OVALS AND CYLINDERS TO FLESH OUT THE FIGURE. SIMPLE SHAPES ARE THE BUILDING BLOCKS OF ANY GREAT SUPER HERO (AND SUPER STRENGTH AND SPEED HELP, TOO!).

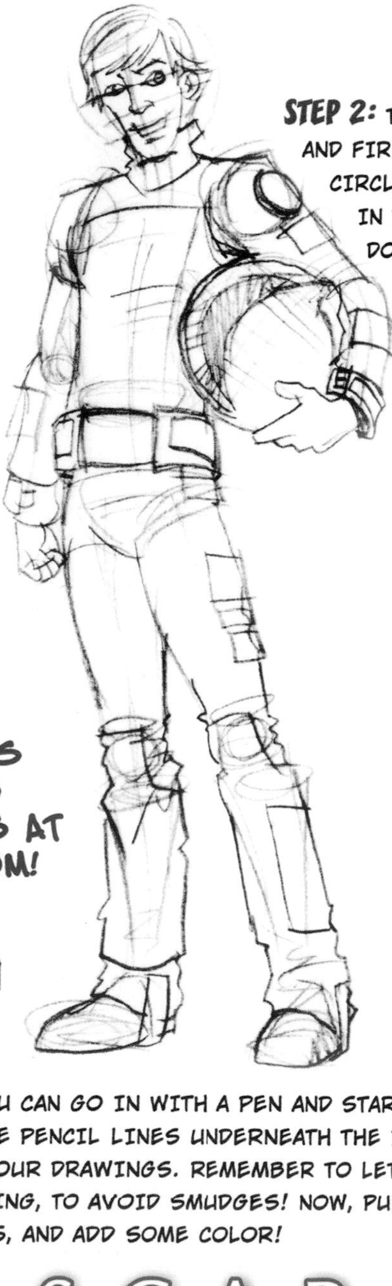

STEP 2: TIME TO FLESH OUT JIMMY'S BODY AND FIRE SUIT. USE GUIDELINES TO ADD CIRCLES FOR HIS EYES. START FILLING IN THE HAIR, AND CLOTHING, AND DON'T FORGET THE HELMET!

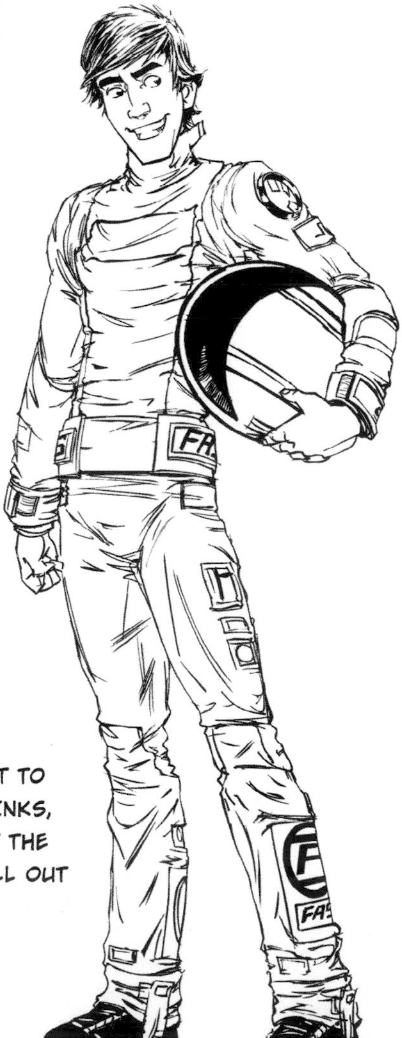
FA
FA

YOU CAN FIND ORE NASCAR HEROES HOW-TO'S, COLORING ETS AND ACTIVITIES AT TARBRIDGEMEDIA.COM!

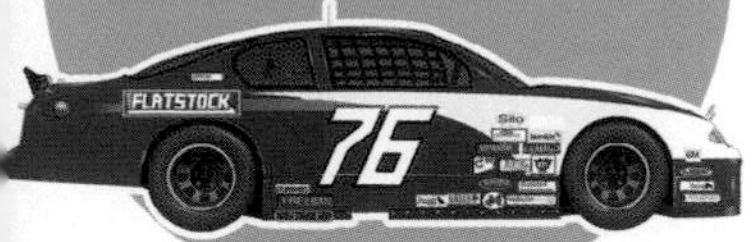
FLATSTOCK
76

STEP 3: AT THIS POINT, YOU CAN GO IN WITH A PEN AND START TO INK THE FIGURE. ERASE THE PENCIL LINES UNDERNEATH THE INKS, FIXING ANY MISTAKES IN YOUR DRAWINGS. REMEMBER TO LET THE PEN INK DRY BEFORE ERASING, TO AVOID SMUDGES! NOW, PULL OUT YOUR MARKERS OR CRAYONS, AND ADD SOME COLOR!

NASCAR LIBRARY COLLECTION

NASCAR HEROES

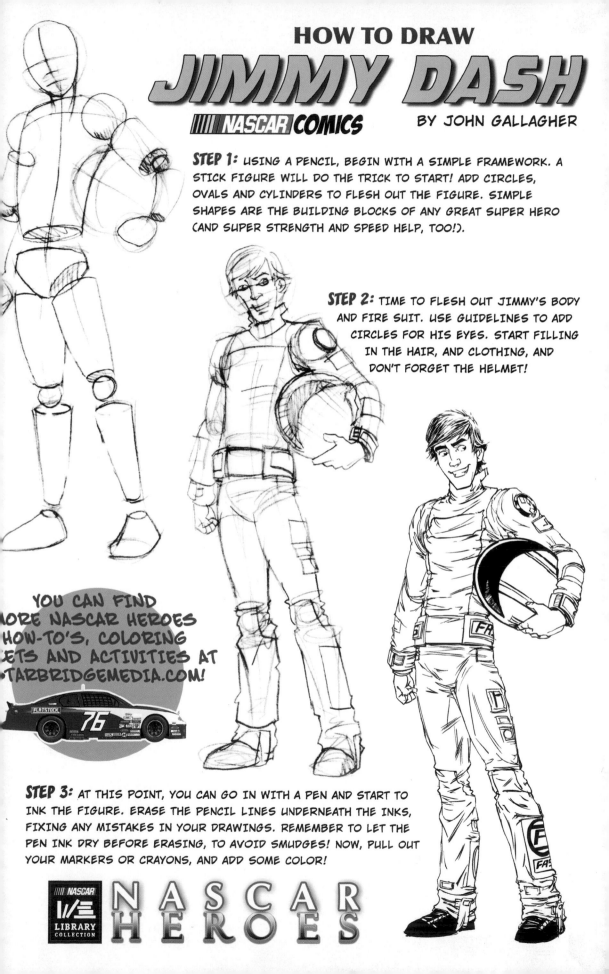

HOW TO DRAW NASCAR COMICS

JACK DIESEL'S NO. 63

BY JOHN GALLAGHER

SURE, JACK DIESEL'S A BAD GUY, BUT HE'S GOT A SET OF WHEELS THAT MAKE HIM A NASCAR SUPERSTAR! HERE'S A QUICK GUIDE ON HOW YOU CAN DRAW JACK'S RIDE!

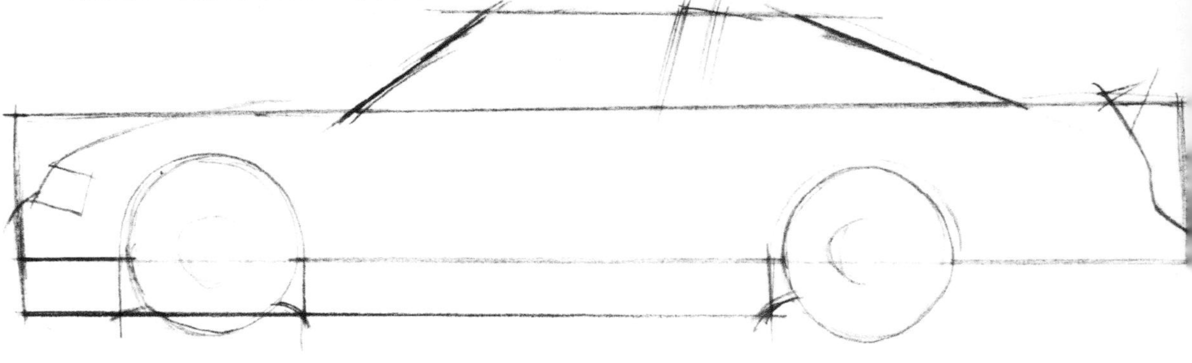

STEP 1: START OFF BY DRAWING A SERIES OF BOXES, SUGGESTING THE SHAPE OF THE CAR AND TIRES. IT'S LIKE CREATING A SHAPE WITH BUILDING BLOCKS, THEN CARVING AWAY AT THE SHAPE INSIDE. YOU CAN DO THIS FREEHAND, OR WITH A RULER, DEPENDING ON HOW "TIGHT" YOU WANT YOUR DRAWING!

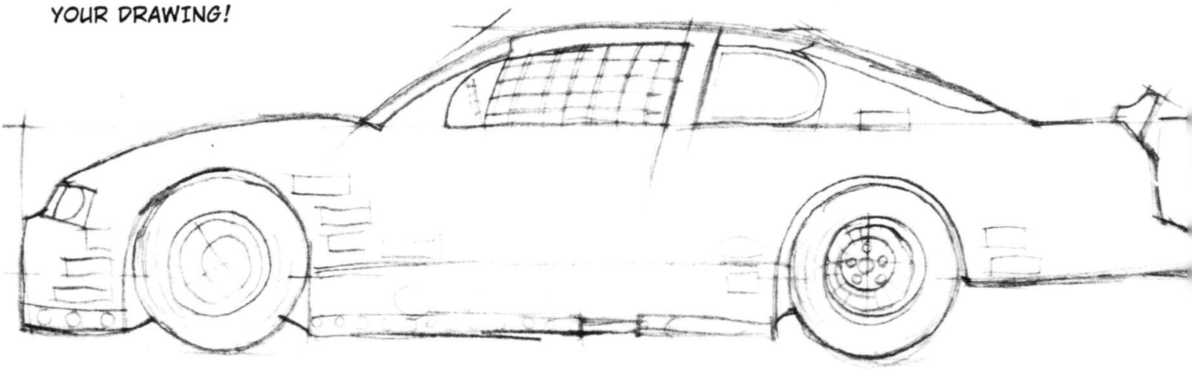

STEP 2: NOW, START TO ZERO IN ON THE SHAPE OF THE CAR FRONT, WINDOWS, TIRES, AND REAR SPOILER. THEN, YOU'LL WANT TO ADD THE DETAILS THAT MAKE A NASCAR UNIQUE, LIKE DECALS, NUMBERS, AND RIVETS!

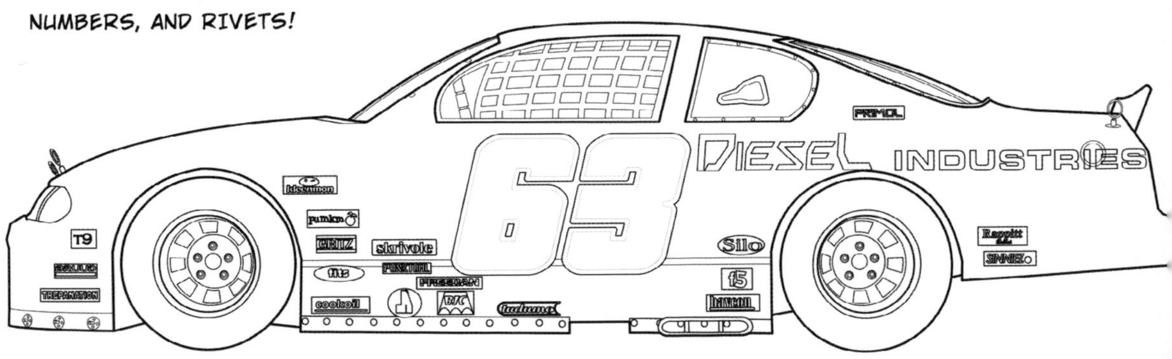
63
DIESEL
INDUSTRIES
PRIMOL
T9
Silo
f5
cookoil

STEP 3: AT THIS POINT, YOU CAN GO IN WITH A PEN AND START TO INK THE CAR, REALLY SHARPENING THE IMAGE! ERASE THE PENCIL LINES UNDERNEATH THE INKS, FIXING ANY MISTAKES IN YOUR DRAWING. GIVE THE CAR THE NUMBER OF YOUR FAVORITE DRIVE (BUT DON'T TELL JACK!), AND ADD SOME COLOR! NOW YOUR DRAWING IS READY TO RACE!

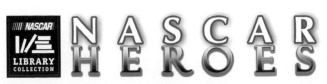